PILGRIM

PILGRIM

RAY HOGAN

DOUBLEDAY & COMPANY, INC.

GARDEN CITY, NEW YORK

1980

With the exception of actual historical personages, all of
the characters in this book are fictitious, and any resem-
blance to actual persons, living or dead, is purely coin-
cidental.

ISBN: 0-385-15630-8
Library of Congress Catalog Card Number 79-7714

for
the Walkers—Vicki, Terry, Ericka, and Kristin

PILGRIM

The quick hammer of oncoming horses reached him as he was climbing the hill. He frowned, turning his dark, brooding features into a study of resentment, and then, raking the sorrel he was riding with his blunted spurs, sent the big gelding lunging up the remainder of the slope.

Gaining the grass-covered, tree-shaded crest of the hill, he halted. It was a posse; there was no doubt of that. What he was unsure of was whether the riders were trailing him or not.

He sat straight and quiet in the saddle listening intently to the drumming of hoofs coming to him from somewhere along the foot of the grade. That he was a tall man was apparent, and when he brushed his weather-stained, warped-brim hat to the back of his head with a gloved hand, he exposed a thatch of thick auburn hair that was badly in need of trimming.

His eyes, fixed on the area below, were light—a chilled-ice blue some termed them—and contained a brittle kind of intensity and were shadowed by full, dark brows. A down-curving mustache partially concealed the hard, thin line of his mouth while his chin and jaw were stubbled with a neglected growth of blue-black whiskers.

Twin, bone-handled pistols hung from crossed belts encircling his lean waist, and red sleeve garters held the cuffs of his white shirt well clear of his hands so that, should the need arise, there would be nothing to hinder his long fingers from making quick use of the weapons. He wore ordinary brown twill pants, the legs of which were tucked into scarred, black boots. A red bandanna, loosely rolled, was around his neck, and there was about him overall a lethal sort of remoteness that bordered on sullenness.

Abruptly his shoulders came forward. A hundred yards or so below two riders had burst into view, were rushing on. Moments later a half-dozen additional men broke out of the ragged oak brush in close pursuit.

The posse was after the two riders—not him. He shrugged. His lank shape relaxed slightly, and twisting half around, he reached into the left-hand saddlebag and drew forth a half-full bottle of whiskey. Tipping it to his lips, he had a long, satisfying drink and, then sighing, restored the bottle to its place inside the leather pouch.

Wiping his mouth with the back of a hand, he let his glance once more probe the trail at the foot of the hill. There was no sign of the two riders, or of the posse. The latter were Circle M ranch cowhands, he reckoned. He'd been on Circle M range since early morning and it was now midday. But it would be something other than just trespassing that instigated the chase he had witnessed; it would have been a more serious matter.

Sleeving away the sweat collecting on his forehead, he restored his hat to proper eye-shielding position and clucked the sorrel into motion. The Texas sun was hot and the sooner he reached a town—there was certain to be one somewhere close by—the sooner he'd find the cool inside of a saloon where he could settle back and enjoy a few hours ease before riding on.

"Wait!"

The wild, desperate plea came from beyond a stand of mesquite a dozen yards ahead. He roweled the sorrel again, lightly, and set the horse to trotting toward the brush. Halting there, he again leaned forward, looked down into a small hollow. The posse had caught up with the two men they were chasing.

Evidently there was but one of the pair involved in the trouble, whatever it was. He was standing alone in a ring of mounted men while his partner, off his saddle also, waited with their horses a short distance away.

It was too far to hear what was being said, but the evident leader of the posse, a large, important-looking individual wearing a high-crowned, white hat, black leather vest, gray plaid shirt with string tie, striped pants, and fancy boots, was leveling a finger at the man inside the circle and speaking angrily. The rider, arms folded across his chest and head down, was making no reply; he simply stood quietly and took the berating.

With his features inscrutable, the tall man on the sorrel watched with no more than ordinary interest. As was the unwritten code of the country, no man interfered in another's business. The fellow in the tall, white hat, probably the owner of the Circle M, was having his say in no uncertain terms to the man before him, who, in some way, had committed a wrong. He could be an unwelcome squatter—a nuisance thief who purloined a steer for his own table now and then, or he could be an out-and-out rustler. The latter was doubtful, however. On such occasions little time was wasted in conversation; it was mostly activity involving a rope, the party concerned, and a convenient tree.

The odds were bad for the man pinned within the circle of riders—six to his one if the friend waiting off to the side wasn't counted. But there was nothing new in that. From the moment of his birth a man assumed risks in one form or another. Sometimes things worked out in his favor, other times, like cards in a poker game, they fell wrong. As for himself, he'd long ago learned that there was very little that was certain in life, that there were no guarantees, and that a—

The abrupt, sharp crack of a gunshot cut into his thoughts and sent an echo rolling across the draws and wooded hills. A second shot followed quickly. The big man in the white hat had suddenly drawn his pistol and put two bullets into the one inside the circle.

All was quiet below after that, with the mounted men remaining motionless as they stared at the sprawled figure before them. And then the big man in the white hat, small streamers of gunsmoke still hanging about him, threw some parting words at the fallen rider's partner, raised his hand in signal to his followers, wheeled, and led them off into the brush.

For a long minute the man on the sorrel at the top of the hill, unmoved by the drama that had taken place below, continued to consider the situation. His expression had scarcely changed when the shooting had erupted; it was as if such was a common incident, a familiar act that stirred him not at all emotionally.

Finally, he rocked back in his saddle and, swinging the sorrel about, headed down the slope for the hollow.

2

As he rode into the clearing, the rider who had been standing off to one side with the horses was bending over the body of his friend, sprawled limply on the short grass. At the sound of the sorrel's approach, he glanced up quickly. There was fear in his eyes.

"Friend—"

The rider's shoulders slumped in relief at the greeting. The tautness faded from his leathery features. He shook his head.

"Old Cain killed him—shot him dead," he said heavily. "You see it? He killed Pete."

The tall man nodded, his hooded eyes and the remoteness of his expression revealing nothing. "He have it coming?"

The rider, a working cowhand from his garb, about thirty, with a dark, narrow face, frowned and drew himself upright.

"Wouldn't be knowing about that. Anyways, since when does Cain Madison need a reason to do anything?"

"There was a lot of talking going on. Must've been some kind of a reason—"

The cowhand spat. "You sure ain't from around here, friend, else you wouldn't say a fool thing like that! Mind telling me who you are?"

The tall man looked to the west out over the flats,

thrusting endlessly toward the horizon. He seemed to be considering the impertinence of the question, and then, as if deciding it was of small consequence, he shrugged.

"Rutledge—John Rutledge," he said. "And you're right —I'm not from around here. Who's the dead man?"

"Name's Pete Lynch—sort of a friend of mine. I'm Noah Webb."

"The big man wearing a white hat—I take it he's Cain Madison."

"Just who he is—and them was some of his hired hands with him—hard cases every last one of them. He don't go no place nowadays without them to back him up."

"We on his range—Circle M?"

Webb nodded and wiped at the sweat on his face with the back of a hand. "Sure are. Cain owns so dang much range around here now that a man can't hardly get off it."

"That what the trouble was between Lynch and Madison?"

"Nope, not exactly. Cain was accusing Pete of rustling his steers—a couple at a time, butchering them and then selling them to a meat market."

Rutledge came slowly off his horse. Removing his hat, he edged into the shade being thrown by a small syca-more.

"Was he?"

"Hell, I don't think Pete was that dumb! I don't figure him touching a Circle M cow with a ten-foot pole!"

"Something made Madison think he did," Rutledge said. His voice was low, his words distinct and precisely enunciated.

"Well, I ain't saying for certain Pete didn't," Webb said, relenting in his stand. "He was owing money around —and there's a woman somewheres he's been keeping up.

I know he was needing cash—but I just can't see him rustling Cain Madison's cows to get it. Somebody else's maybe, but not Circle M stuff."

"Didn't he work for somebody?"

"Yeh, the widow. Didn't make hardly nothing there, howsomever."

"The widow?"

"Hetty Judson. Got herself a little spread on up the way a few miles. Having it mighty hard herself—she was only paying Pete four bits a day and found."

Rutledge stirred and placed his attention on Lynch's body. "Well, whatever the reason for it, he's dead and out of it now."

Webb scrubbed at the stubble on his jaw. "That's for sure—he don't have to do no fretting now. But, damn it, I still can't figure him for a rustler! I got a hunch it's all hooked up with Cain trying to force the widow's hand—"

"To do what—sell out to him?"

"Yep, that's what he's been trying to do ever since he come here and started buying up the little outfits and spreading out."

John Rutledge shook his head slowly. It was the same old story—the big rancher driving out the small ones, along with the homesteaders, and taking over their land for his own use. It never seemed to matter how much range they had or if they needed additional acreage, they always wanted more—and were never satisfied. He knew —he'd worked for a few men like Cain Madison farther south, in Texas.

"It's a sad story," he murmured dryly, "but it's nothing new."

Webb glanced at Rutledge curiously, his forehead knotted into a frown. "Got to say you're mighty offhand about all this, mister! There's a man laying there dead. Don't that mean nothing to you?"

Rutledge's wide shoulders stirred indifferently. "We've all got to die someday—what's the difference when?" He paused and smiled faintly at Webb. "What do you aim to do with him—bury him right here?"

Noah Webb considered that briefly, and then came to the question. "Nope, got to load him up on his horse and take him to the widow. Was what Madison told me to do —tote him up to her place. I'm to tell her what happened and why he's dead and say that it don't end there—and then I'm to get the hell out of the country."

A thin smile again cracked John Rutledge's lips. "And you're doing it—just like he said?"

"You can bet your bottom dollar I am!" Webb replied with feeling. "I ain't fool enough to buck Cain Madison or any of that hard-case bunch that works for him! And that includes that boy of his'n, too—Clint. Soon as I get shed of Pete I'm lining out for Kansas. Got some friends up that-away that'll help me get a job."

Nearby in the brush a camp robber jay scolded noisily. Rutledge listened to the bird's sharp rebuke for a few moments, and then nodded. "Expect you're being smart. I don't figure you for a man who'd buck the odds."

"And you'd sure as hell be right when it comes to Cain Madison!" Webb declared. "There ain't no sense going up against him. A man best forget about it because he ain't got a chance. . . . Say, Rutledge, which way are you heading? Maybe we could ride together a spell if you're pointing east?"

"No, riding west—for New Mexico or maybe on to Arizona. Not sure exactly where I'll wind up."

Webb's features broke into a hopeful grin. "Then maybe you can do me a big favor—a mighty big one!"

The jay was at it again, flitting erratically in and out of the brush, chattering and scolding loudly. Rutledge once more paused to listen and then reaching into his saddlebag, obtained his bottle of whiskey. Uncorking the bottle, he passed it first to Webb who took a short drink, grimaced, and returned it. The tall man had his swallow, replaced the container, and put his attention again on the nervously fluttering bird. Evidently there was a nest with young ones nearby.

"You hear me?" Webb pressed.

Rutledge said, "You're asking a favor—that it?"

"Yes, sir. Want to know if you'd mind taking Pete with you and leaving him at the Judson place when you go by."

Rutledge reset his hat, brushed at his mouth, gave the request thought.

"It sure would be a powerful help to me," Webb said anxiously. "Madison told me to get out of the country fast. He knowed me and Pete was friends and I figure he'd about as soon put a bullet in me as draw his next breath—and he probably will if he or any of his bunch runs into me again.

"If you'll do me the favor it'd save me two maybe three miles—and I can be a far piece from here in that much time!"

"Where is the Judson place?"

"About five miles on west, and a bit north. A man can't miss it."

"It on the trail?"

"Nope, but there's a sign saying it's the Judson ranch.

You turn off on the road where it's standing—it'll be to your left—and it'll take you right to the house."

Rutledge remained silent and Webb, taking his hesitancy for indecision, continued hurriedly. "Can get yourself a job there now, too, I expect, if you're looking for work. Cash pay won't be much but the widow feeds good and she's a real pretty woman.

"And there ain't a whole lot of work to it. There's just her and her youngun—a little girl about six or seven—and a few cows. Pete told me the job was a real easy one—and if I wasn't having to pull out, I reckon I'd be going after it myself."

"Not looking for work," Rutledge said bluntly, "specially one nursing cows. Already paid my dues at that kind of living."

"Was only thinking that if you was, it'd be a easy place to sign on," Webb said, crestfallen. "The widow will be needing help."

"Your friend Lynch, there, the only hand she had?"

"Yeh, only one," Noah replied. "And since you don't aim to work for her I might as well tell you why. He was the only man around with guts enough to hire out to her, or maybe it was because he had to have a job, I just can't say for certain. But fact is, Madison's got everybody else scared off, plain afeard to work for her. But," he added, assessing Rutledge with a narrow glance, "I don't reckon you can understand that. I misdoubt you ever let anybody keep you from doing what you wanted."

The tall rider smiled faintly. "That's about the truth of it," he said. "Come on, let's load your friend there crossways on his saddle. Want to tie him down good. I don't aim to have him sliding off somewhere along the trail."

"Yes, sir, Mr. Rutledge!" Noah Webb said happily, hurrying to Pete Lynch's horse. "I sure am more than obliged to you for doing me this favor. Yes, sir, I sure am!"

3

A cattle grower couldn't ask for a more ideal country in which to raise beef, Rutledge thought as he rode slowly along the trail with the horse packing Pete Lynch's body following close behind. The grass was lush and plentiful, and there were indications of springs bursting forth in numerous places, while small groves of trees, offering shade from the hot sun, were scattered about across the land as if by design.

He supposed he could understand Cain Madison's desire to own it all. He had just come from a couple of years of violence and bloodshed that sprang from just such greed. It had been a time of rancher against rancher, of rancher against homesteader—and friend against friend.

Rutledge, thanks to his skill with a pistol, had hired on to one of the larger outfits as a gunman. It wasn't that he held a particular brief for the owner of the spread or that he had anything against the opposition, it was only that it promised danger and heady excitement—and relief from a past that, despite gambling and constant liquor, he could not erase from his mind.

For a while it was a series of shootings and surprise attacks, of riding hard and fast, of narrow escapes not only from opposing forces but the law as well—law that included not just town and county officers but also the Texas Rangers. And strangely enough it was a lawman, a deputy sheriff, leading a prisoner into an ambush that brought the bloody affair to an end.

Rutledge—he did not call himself by that name in those days—joined with the murdered man's friends and relatives to institute a vengeful search for the dozen or so bushwhackers who had participated in the senseless killing. The sheriff, hoping perhaps to stem the wave of bloodshed before it got underway, sent for the leaders of the search to come to his office and talk over the situation.

However, before the two men summoned reached town where the sheriff awaited them, they also encountered an ambush and one of them was killed. The escaping member, wounded, managed to rejoin the rest of the avenging party and all retired to the hills to lie low for a few days.

It wasn't long until they were ready to move again—this time in small groups dispatched to seek out and kill specific persons. Rutledge grinned tightly as he recalled the man he and a friend were assigned to take care of. They had found him—a cheap, tinhorn gambler—at a place called Comanche Creek. The shoot-out had been brief, and when it was over they had accomplished, without injury to themselves, the job they had been sent to do.

Elsewhere in the area, other factions of the revenge party had been fulfilling their deadly missions with cold efficiency and a tide of violence suddenly was flowing across the land.

Rutledge and another member were dispatched on a second errand, this time to track down and eliminate one of the last participants in the ambush—many others had fled the state when retribution began to overtake them. They found him, or at least the one whom they were told was him. A shoot-out ensued, but their information had been in error and they killed the brother of the man they sought. Before they could ride off into the brush to continue the search, they were trapped by lawmen and thrown in jail.

Fortunately the revenge party was long on friends. Most of the persons in the counties involved in the war were sympathetic and believed that the law favored the opposition. Thus that very first night a crowd began to assemble in the town with the avowed intent of breaking Rutledge and his partner out of jail.

Determined to prevent such, the marshal secretly moved his prisoners to the lockup in the capital city of Austin. It was to no purpose. Another crowd gathered and the lawman was again forced to transfer his charges, this time to a county jail some distance away. It was a waste of energy. A third group of sympathizers assembled, this time were successful, and Rutledge and his friend escaped into the hills.

It was a difficult period for John Rutledge. With nothing to do but remain in hiding with a man he cared little for as a companion, he spent endless hours drinking and mulling over the past, thinking about Lacey, the girl who haunted his mind, and how it might have been had she lived to fulfill their plans and dreams.

The promise of the future had been beyond compare: a generous stake from his well-to-do family with which to start a life of their own and realize the hope of building an empire, of attaining high public office, of becoming a factor in the building of the land. But then came the collapse, the shattering of the dream.

Thus it was not unexpected when Rutledge, unable to stand his own thoughts any longer, insisted they ride out sooner than was prudent, and rode boldly back to the original meeting place of the revenge group, rejoined those who were still around, and resumed the search for the last of the bushwhackers.

Most of them, however, were either already dead or had departed for safer climes, and the party began gradually to break up with members going their separate ways. Rutledge chose to make Kansas his destination.

Unfortunately, his contempt for lawmen was his nemesis. Instead of riding on to Dodge City as he'd planned, he delayed and got involved in a drinking bout at the ranch of a friend. It cost him his freedom; the Rangers, hearing of his presence, closed in and, making their arrest, took him back to the point where the violence had started. There he was charged with the murder of one of the bushwhackers and locked in jail to await trial.

Paradoxically, it was his old enemy, the law, which brought about his release from the charge. At the time of the killing, John Rutledge had been securely behind bars in the jail of a nearby county and therefore could not possibly have been involved. Thus he was freed.

But he realized he would not remain so for long. There were other killings in which he had participated that the Rangers and local lawmen, now reinforced by a wave of public indignation, would like to saddle him with—and he was too smart a gambler to think he could beat the odds. Passing along the word that he was going on to Dodge City, as planned, he reversed his course and struck west for the adjoining territory of New Mexico.

Never one to avoid trouble—on the contrary being a man who only too often sought it—he nevertheless had no intentions of delivering himself into the hands of the law.

Thus on his journey from deep south Texas he had used care not usual but necessary, staying off the main trails and going into settlements only for supplies and whiskey replenishment—his one ally against the recurring memory of Lacey and the past.

That was all there was left for John Rutledge in life— the need and the means by which to forget, which did include on occasion the perusal of some of his favorite books—classics—taken when he rode away from home and struck out on his own seeking oblivion.

Whiskey, violence, danger—those were the factors that guided his existence, while the major element, disillusionment, lying deep in his subconscious, hoped and prayed for a bullet that one day would bring an end to it all.

But, as was the inexplicable rule in the majority of such instances, those who by reckless and foolhardy action sought death never found it. John Rutledge had weathered a dozen or more bloody gunfights and had seen friends drop at his side while he himself never suffered more than simple wounds. He tried to understand it, struggled to find an explanation in the words of the wise men who wrote the books he read. He discovered only that they, too, were puzzled. Thus, as time wore on, he had no choice but to accept his lot and—

Rutledge slowed the sorrel, eyes on a slanting pole ahead on the trail. The words JUDSON'S RANCH were in faded letters on the sign that topped its height.

He nodded, reached for his bottle, and had a satisfying drink. Here was where he would discharge the favor he'd promised Noah Webb; he'd rid himself of the body of Pete Lynch, explain to the widow what had happened, and then be on his way. It should take no more than an hour—probably less.

Roweling the sorrel, Rutledge continued, came to the fork, and swung off the trail onto the narrow, brush-lined lane that led toward the hills visible against the distant horizon in the west. The Judson place looked good; he could not help but note the fact, although there was some indication of neglect. That was easily explained, he guessed, by the fact that the Judson woman was a widow and had great difficulty in hiring help.

The lane bent and Rutledge found himself at the edge of a small clearing. The house, long and low with what appeared to be a fence on its roof, was on ahead. He could see no one around, no one at the house or anywhere about the lesser sheds and structures and corrals beyond it. He reckoned he'd just have to unload Lynch's body, lay it on the porch, and ride on if he couldn't raise anyone.

That didn't sound exactly right to him—just leaving a dead body for the woman to find. But there were reasons why he'd as soon move right on. He had made up his mind to go to New Mexico, and certainly he wasn't going to let himself be rung in on another range war such as he'd gone through down in south Texas! The idea of new country appealed to him—a place where he could start over and not be bothered by small-town marshals and county sheriffs sniffing at his heels.

He continued, slowly walking the sorrel and the trailing buckskin with its grisly burden. There'd be somebody around; they'd not leave the place unattended, not at that hour of the day.

The sudden sharp crack of a rifle and the simultaneous spurt of dust off the lane just ahead of him brought Rutledge to a quick stop and sent a hand reaching for one of the pistols at his hips. A wry, angry grin split his mouth. There was someone there, all right—someone making it plenty plain that he was unwelcome.

4

Rutledge swung down from his saddle, his movements stiff, angry. "Hold up!" he shouted, raising a hand. "Friend!"

Hesitating briefly for that bit of information to register, he started forward again, leading the horses at a slow pace. He had taken no more than two strides when the rifle spat once more, reawakening the echoes and sending them rolling across the flats anew.

"Damn it!" he yelled in exasperation. "I've come friendly! Hold your fire!"

Repeating the slight delay, he lifted both hands above his head and, with the reins of the sorrel laced between his fingers, resumed his deliberate approach. The rifle barked its spiteful warning for a third time.

Rutledge pulled up short. Lowering his arms, he shook his head. The hell with it! Why should he risk his life performing a favor for a stranger? He'd lead the buckskin with Pete Lynch's body tied onto it out in front, give the horse a good slap on the rump, and send him on in. Let the widow Judson, or whoever the hell it was sniping at him, take it from there.

Sure, the woman should be told what had happened, how Lynch had died and such, and he should convey the threat implied in Cain Madison's words—but if she wouldn't let him get near enough to talk, he'd just let it slide. If he was going to catch a bullet, he wanted it to be over something of consequence and not because some jittery, fool woman thought he—

The rifle cracked again, drilling a bullet into the dark, red soil a scant yard from his foot. That was a final warning, he reckoned, since he had not been moving. It had but one meaning: get out.

Rutledge started to wheel, untie the lead rope attached to the buckskin, and free him. A faint rustling in the brush and the muted thud of a horse's hoofs brought him to quick alert. He gave no indication that he had heard, however, but continued to work at the knot in the buckskin's tether—doing so with his left hand in order to leave the right, hovering near the pistol on that side, unencumbered.

The noise ceased. The rider had halted, was probably dismounting and closing in on foot. Cool, Rutledge continued to work at the buckskin's rope. Abruptly it came free. Wheeling casually, the tall rider began to gather it in, looping it into a coil and returning it to its thong on his saddle. His attention was not wholly on the task. As he pulled the strip of leather cord tight about the rope, he was keeping a sharp watch from the tail of an eye on the brush where he had heard the oncoming horse.

Suddenly a figure stepped into view. Rutledge's tensed shoulders relented. A hard grin pulled at his mouth.

"Lady, that's a damn good way to get your head blown off!" he snapped.

The woman shrugged. "Not unless you're a lot faster at drawing than I think," she said quietly, waggling the pistol she held in her hand. It was cocked and pointed at him. "I was ready."

She paused, glanced at the body hung across the buckskin, and frowned. Tall, about his own age, Rutledge figured. She had dark hair, deep-blue eyes, and appeared to be well built despite the old and faded pair of denim pants and bulky plaid shirt she was wearing. An equally aged hat was on her head, and the scarred boots encasing her feet looked a bit large.

"Who's this—and why'd you bring him here?"

"Doing a fellow named Webb a favor. Said the man worked for you—if you're the widow Judson."

"I'm Hetty Judson," she replied, still cool. "You haven't said who you are."

"Name's John Rutledge. I'm just riding through on my way to—"

"Who'd you say the dead man was?" Hetty cut in impatiently. Her hair had been pulled up beneath the old hat, but it had come loose in places and now several strands hung down about her face and neck.

"Was on my way to New Mexico," Rutledge continued, ignoring the interruption, "and I didn't say who he was. Just keep your shirt on for a bit and I'll get to it."

Hetty Judson glanced toward the house, then, crossing her arms over her chest, stared at him. "Well, do it! I've got plenty of other things to do besides stand here."

"Goes for me, too," Rutledge replied, equally brusque. "Man there's Pete Lynch. Was shot down by Cain Madison. His friend Webb was in a hurry to get out of the country and asked me to leave the body here when I rode by. I've done that, madam, so it's so long!"

As Rutledge turned, thrust a foot into a stirrup, Hetty came forward impulsively. "No—wait! I didn't aim to be short with you. It's just that things just won't go right and I've been having so much trouble, and I can't seem to

make any headway at all—at anything. Please tell me
what happened."

There was no complaint in the woman's voice, only a
note of impatience. Holstering the pistol and circling, she
came around to the off side of the buckskin to where she
could see the features of the dead man. Gazing at the
slack face for a few moments, she sighed. "Poor Pete. He
never was much as help goes but he did what he could—
and he certainly didn't deserve killing. Do you know why
Madison shot him?"

"Claimed Lynch had been rustling some of his steers—a
couple at a time and then selling the meat to a butcher
somewhere."

"Pete?" Hetty echoed. "I don't mean to bad-mouth him
now that he's dead, but I don't think he had enough
gumption to do that. Did Cain Madison have proof?"

Rutledge's shoulders stirred. "Wouldn't know. I wasn't
in on the shooting that much. Webb didn't seem to think
there was anything to it, but he did say that Lynch was
owing money around."

"Who to?"

"Never said. He just didn't rule out the idea that Lynch
might be doing it since he was needing cash."

"Pete was always broke," the woman said, looking off
toward the house again. "Told me that he was planning
to get married once he got on his feet. Some girl living
north of town. I'd sure like to know for sure if he was
rustling."

"I reckon that's something nobody'll ever know for sure
now since he's the only one who could answer the question," Rutledge said, also glancing to the house.

He was wondering who had fired the rifle shots at him.
Hetty Judson had been too near and had been off in a

different direction, so it could not have been her—and there was no husband or hired help, only a child, a girl of six or seven, Webb had said, living there besides the widow. Could she have been the one using the rifle?

"Webb wanted me to tell you, too, that Madison said this wasn't the end of it far as you're concerned. I took that to be a warning."

Hetty's full, dark brows lifted and fell. "Just what it was, but it's not the first. He's been warning me in one way or another ever since I've—we've—been here. Did you see the shooting?"

Rutledge said, "Yes, was off a piece, however. Had heard horses coming up fast. Thought at first it was a posse looking for me."

"The law after you?"

"More or less," Rutledge drawled. "I pulled up, watched them ride by, then a bit later I saw them again. Had stopped in a little coulee—a half a dozen men and this fellow Madison. Had shaped a circle and Lynch was standing in the middle of it. Madison was raising hell with him—over the rustling, I expect. Webb was off to one side with his horse and the buckskin there. Then Madison pulled his gun and shot Lynch."

Hetty was frowning angrily. "You—you just sat there and let Cain Madison murder Pete without trying to stop him? Couldn't you see what was happening, that Cain and his bunch of hard cases had trapped Pete and were aiming to kill him?"

Rutledge brushed his hat to the back of his head and wiped at the sweat on his forehead. "First off," he began patiently, "I was too far off to know what it was all about. Second, it sure wasn't any of my business. I don't know how long you've lived in this country, but the rule here is that a man keeps his nose out of another man's business—"

"Even if he's about to murder somebody?"

"Murder? Now, maybe Lynch was a rustler. Could be Cain Madison had the right to do what he did. It's understood that a rancher can hang or shoot a rustler. That's another rule you best get used to—"

"Rule!" Hetty Judson exploded. "You men and your damned rules and codes! It's all a lot of poppycock!"

"Could be," Rutledge said, and again turned to mount his horse. "Best I be riding on. I've done what I told Webb I would."

"Oh, please—just a moment!" Hetty said hurriedly, her tone contrite, as before. "I didn't mean what I said. I know that it has to be that way out here or the outlaws would soon take over. I'm sorry—"

"Forget it. I understand."

"I'd like to ask you something; will you do *me* a favor now?"

Rutledge considered the woman with cool, level eyes. She was a right pretty woman as Noah Webb had said, and he reckoned he could overlook her snappish ways on that account alone. But he wasn't about to get involved in her problems with Cain Madison.

"Depends—"

"It's Pete there—will you help me bury him?"

Rutledge gave the request a moment's thought. He glanced up at the sun. Another hour wouldn't make any difference, he supposed.

"Lead the way," he said, nodding.

5

Hetty Judson cut back into the brush and within a few moments returned astride a thick-bodied little bay. Rutledge, again in the saddle, wheeled in behind her as she rode past. Then, in single file, they continued along the lane together to the house.

As they came into the yard the door of the house opened and a child—the girl of six or seven that Noah Webb had mentioned—came out onto the porch. Hetty smiled at her and nodded to Rutledge.

"This is my daughter, Willa," she said, and as the girl halted abruptly, eyes fixed on the body of Lynch, added: "It's Pete, honey. He had some trouble with Cain Madison. We're going to bury him up near your papa."

Willa, a serious-faced miniature of her mother, only stared.

"This is Mr. Rutledge. He's going to help me," the woman continued.

The girl turned to the tall rider.

"You're a pretty good shooter—if you were the one with the rifle," Rutledge said.

Willa considered him blankly for a long breath and then turned and went back into the house.

Hetty smiled wanly and shook her head. "You'll have to excuse her. She's been like that ever since her daddy was killed—kind of resentful where men are concerned. It's as if she blames all men for his death."

"Not hard to understand," Rutledge said, "but I expect she'll get over it."

"In time, I'm sure," Hetty said. "I'll fetch a spade, and something to wrap Pete in."

Rutledge nodded and waited while the woman went into a nearby shed to return quickly with the items mentioned. "She stay here alone?" he asked.

Hetty said, "She has to. I haven't been able to hire a housekeeper—even if I had the cash to do so."

"Seems a bit risky, considering the way Madison feels—"

"He wouldn't dare hurt her," the woman said, throwing the piece of canvas she had obtained over Pete Lynch's body and wedging the spade under the stirrup flap. "That's some of your code that I approve of: a man just doesn't hurt a child. Anyway, Willa knows to stay inside the house, locked up, when I'm not around. I've taught her to use a rifle, to start shooting at anybody she sees coming toward the house unless she knows who they are and that they're friends—and there's damn few of them."

"She stopped me for certain," Rutledge said with a grin. "Could she hit somebody if she wanted to?"

"I don't know. The need hasn't come up yet but I expect she could," Hetty replied as they moved out across the yard. "She rests the gun on the sill of the window. It steadies her aim and checks some of the kick."

Rutledge had glanced to the roof of the house, curious as to the fence arrangement on its forward corner. He saw it was a roof deck, and guessed the Judsons had taken enjoyment from the view of the surrounding country available to them from that higher elevation.

"You can see the slope over there," Hetty said, pointing

to the family cemetery, a square plot of ground enclosed
by rocks and exhibiting a lone grave marker. "I'll meet
you there. I want to get another spade."

Rutledge gave no sign that he had heard, merely
clucked to his horse and guided him, with Lynch's buckskin trailing, toward the area. Reaching there he drew up
to a fairly large chinaberry tree that spread its shade
across the slope and, halting, dismounted. Tying the sorrel and the buckskin to the tree, he stepped up to the latter, laid the tarp and spade aside, and began to release
the rope that held Lynch's body in place.

Hetty Judson arrived moments later with the extra
spade she had gone for. Picking up the canvas and the
other tool, she carried all into the stone-marked enclosure.
Spreading the tarp on the grassy ground, she crossed to a
far corner of the area, marked off a grave, and began to
dig. Rutledge, lifting Lynch's body off the horse and carrying it to where Hetty had laid the canvas, lowered the
man onto it and then wrapped it about him.

Wheeling, he sighed, took up the other spade, and
moving to where the woman was working steadily, began
to assist her. Chopping and ricking wood and using a
spade were two things in life John Rutledge disliked in-
tensely, and his regret at having granted a favor to Noah
Webb had now grown to major proportions. But he said
nothing about it; he'd given his word and he'd stand by it.

Finally they had a trench large enough in the soft soil.
Together they lifted the wrapped body of Pete Lynch
and placed it in the grave. Hetty, waved off by Rutledge,
stood aside while he filled in the loose earth, mounded it,
and patted it smooth with his spade. That done, he
brushed away the accumulation of sweat on his forehead
and stepped clear.

"Two graves now," the woman murmured, "and Cain Madison's to blame for both of them."

Rutledge, leaning his spade against a nearby clump of redberry, removed his gloves and crossed to his horse. Reaching into a saddlebag, he produced his bottle of whiskey and, returning, pulled the cork and offered the liquor to Hetty. She smiled, shook her head, and sat down on one of the larger stones that made up the border.

"Expect it's all right with you if I have one," Rutledge said, making it a statement rather than a question. "The business end of a shovel's not exactly my long suit."

Again Hetty smiled. "I guessed as much. Go right ahead."

Rutledge had his swallow, restored the bottle to its place on his saddle, and taking a black stogie from a leather case in his shirt pocket, struck a match to the weed and puffed it into life. He moved back to her.

"You say Madison killed your husband, too?"

Hetty nodded. "Far as I'm concerned he did, either pulling the trigger himself or telling one of his hired hands to do it."

"How'd it happen?"

Hetty glanced off, then looked directly at him. He had thought earlier that she was most attractive and realized now as she faced him—features calm, dark eyes a deep, quiet blue, soft hair slightly visible about her head where it was able to escape the confines of the old hat—that she actually was a beautiful woman. It occurred to him then that it hardly seemed right that one so lovely should be burdened with so much trouble; but trouble, John Rutledge had learned long ago, was no respecter of persons—it came to everyone.

"You really want to hear about my problems?"

Rutledge shrugged, exhaled a small cloud of smoke, and glanced off toward the small vegetable garden near the house where a meadowlark was whistling cheerfully in the bright, afternoon sunshine.

"Sure, if you're of a mind," he said. "It's going to take a bit of time to get my wind back after that digging."

She smiled at his words. "It'll be good to talk about it. I've never had anyone to tell my story to, up to now."

Rutledge squatted, settled on his haunches, and blew another puff of smoke into the warm, quiet air. "Thought Lynch was a regular hand of yours."

"Guess you could say he was, but he was never around long enough to carry on a conversation with. He was either leaving to do some work or on his way to town."

"Don't you have any neighbors?"

"Not any more. Jack, my husband, and I came here about eight years ago. He had some money left him by his grandfather and since we'd always wanted to come west and try our hand at ranching, we did. Ended up here.

"The place was for sale—an elderly couple owned it, but the man died and the lady wanted to go back to her home somewhere in Ohio. We got the ranch at a fair price and started right in doing what we'd dreamed of— ranching.

"Everything went along fine. Our herd increased and we were able to sell off enough stock to keep us in cash and pay expenses. We had several good neighbors then, and all in all it was a wonderful life.

"Willa was born a couple of years after we got here, and that made things all the better. I remember thinking once that nobody, not in the whole world, could be as contented and happy as we were. But it was just too good to last. It all came to an end."

"Cain Madison," Rutledge said, studying the tip of his cigar.

"Cain Madison," Hetty repeated, a hardness creeping into her voice. "He showed up about four years ago with a pocket full of money. Somebody said he came from Kansas, or maybe it was Nebraska, and that he'd made his fortune there."

The woman paused, her gaze lost in the distance, her lips set to a firm line as she recalled the bitter past. "He bought out our neighbors, the Caswells. They had the largest spread around here. And then he started adding to it by buying up all the small outfits, paying whatever price they asked in hard cash money."

"But you and your husband turned down his offer."

"We did. The price was good, actually more than we'd put in the place, but we had no reason to sell out. Jack and I both loved it here and wanted to stay. I guess that was where we made our mistake—if you can call it a mistake; we stood up to Cain Madison, refused to sell out to him. Doing that cost Jack his life—and me the only man I ever loved."

Hetty's voice had dropped, and there was a hint of tremor in it. Rutledge stirred and shifted his position.

"Can let it go there if you're finding it painful to talk," he said.

The woman shook her head. "No, I think this is what I need. Somebody to sort of unload it all on. It's been bottled up in me for a long time."

"Sometimes it helps," he agreed. "Mind telling me how your husband got killed? He face up to Madison, try to shoot it out with him?"

6

"Jack was ambushed," Hetty Judson said, her eyes partly closed. "He was on his way home from town late one afternoon. As he was coming up the road about a mile from here, he was shot."

"He alone at the time?"

"Yes. There was a man by the name of Gilroy working for us. He was over on our south range and heard the shots. He went to see what it was about, but he was too late to help Jack—he'd been hit four times, probably died instantly. He's the one who brought Jack home."

"Weren't you ever able to get an idea who had done the shooting?"

"Nothing more than that Jack had talked to Cain Madison that morning in town and had again turned down an offer to buy us out. Madison became terribly angry, according to John Granville, the owner of the general store, who overheard their conversation. He said that Cain actually threatened my husband."

"What did the law have to say about it?"

Hetty laughed scornfully. "The law here is Marshal Tom Farwell who's always quick to tell you that his authority ends at the edge of town. I went to him, of course, that very next day and told him all I knew about it and that Madison had been overheard threatening Jack.

"He said he couldn't do anything about it but he did

promise to turn the matter over to the sheriff who had authority over the entire county. And he did—finally. The sheriff rode out to see me about three months after it happened. It was all a waste of time, far as the law is concerned."

Rutledge shrugged and knocked the ash from his cigar tip with a finger. "Law generally works that way, I've found. If it's butter for their own biscuits, you'll get action. If not, they just forget it."

Hetty touched him with a quick glance. "You sound like you don't have much use for the law, either."

"I don't," he said, and let the matter drop. "From what I hear Madison's still trying to buy you out."

"He's never stopped. I could expect to hear from him at least once a week there for a while. He'd come by or send his son, Clint—or maybe it would be Dave Hollander, his foreman. Dave came by pretty often for a time, sort of courted me, although I never did encourage it. And I caught it from the merchants in town, too. Never real strong, just sort of a hint or a suggestion that, being a lone woman, the smart thing would be to sell to Madison.

"I knew he had put them up to it and I felt sorry for them. The Circle M is a big customer, buys a lot of supplies and none of them could afford to lose the business. But I didn't let any of it bother me. Just went right on running the ranch the way Jack and I together had been doing. We had two hired hands at the time, Gilroy and a Mexican fellow named Madrid, who were doing most of the work around. So the only change was the terrible loneliness I felt with Jack gone.

"We'd been through good times and bad times together. We'd hit rock bottom a couple of times and then climbed back up to the top a couple of times, too. We'd suffered and starved and froze and done a lot of laughing together. And you might as well know, we cried a'plenty, too. So at the very first after I realized, fully, that Jack was gone, I found myself facing a big, dark emptiness in which the only bit of sunshine was my little daughter, Willa. Save but for her, nothing seemed worthwhile."

John Rutledge nodded slowly. He had removed the cigar from between his clenched teeth and was staring moodily at its smoldering tip.

"I know," he said quietly. "Nothing can take the place of what a man and woman, together, goes through when they are up against it, have to fight to survive, and win. Hard times push them tight together, builds a sort of bond between them that nobody can ever replace." He paused, looked up at the woman. There was an odd, self-conscious smile on his lips, as if embarrassed by the lengthy speech he had made. Finally, he added: "Seems you didn't give up."

"No, I got a hold of myself and kept things going. Madison changed his tactics. He ran off my hired help, fixed it so's I couldn't get anybody around here to work for me, at least not for long. And then there were the things his cowhands would do—like shoot a steer now and then, or drag up brush to block a water hole. And there were a couple of grass fires they started.

"But I managed to hang on and did the best I could with what I had. I didn't ask any favors from the merchants in town, or anyone else, and I didn't grant any. I let it be known that I'd shoot the first trespasser that set foot on my range and that stopped Madison's cowhands from deviling me.

"Now and then I was able to hire a drifter that was passing through and get things caught up a little, but they were never able to stay long. Sooner or later Madison and his bunch got to them, drove them off. All but Pete Lynch.

"He showed up one day looking for a job—any kind, he said. I told him right off that he could go to work right that minute but that he'd be taking a chance. He wanted to know why and then I told him about Madison. His answer to that was that he'd look out for himself and for me not to worry about him. That's how he went to work for me. He wasn't too good, being slow and not very handy, but he was help and I appreciated having him around.

"I'm sorry Madison caught up with him. He deserved a better end than being murdered for something I don't think he was guilty of. I'm sorry, too, for myself. This has happened right when I need somebody to work. The upper part of my range is hill country. There's a lot of brushy draws and they're full of strays. I've got to round them up, drive them down to the lower range.

"And the calves'll need branding. There won't be many —there never is. The wolves and the big cats always get most of them, but what I will have'll need taking care of."

"With the kind of range I've seen, you ought to have a big calf crop," Rutledge observed. "Cows just naturally get in a family way with such good grazing."

"Should, and I guess they do," Hetty replied with a sigh, "but the tally's always small. Has been for several years."

"And you figure it's because of mountain lions and wolves?"

She nodded. "Seems the only answer. Why? Don't you think that's it?"

Rutledge struck a match to the lifeless butt of his cigar. "Well, I haven't been across all of your range but I never saw any sign of either cats or wolves on the part that I did ride. Could be you've got two-legged varmints helping themselves to your calves."

"Could be," Hetty said doubtfully, "but nobody, or I for that matter—has ever come across any indication of it."

"Probably because you don't have any hired help to look into it. Next man you sign on, tell him to keep an eye on your calves. Take a spring count, see how it jibes later on."

Hetty shrugged. "It wouldn't be hard to run a ranch right if I could hire good men to help out. I just can't do the job alone. About all I can do is keep my head above water—and even if I believe that, I'm fooling myself. Things aren't at a standstill, they're slipping back—going down—going to hell in a hand basket as my husband would say. In a couple more years this ranch will be nothing more than a ruin—the echo of what was once a beautiful dream. Does that sound poetic and high-flown? Maybe it is, but it's true and it's how I feel."

Rutledge smiled understandingly. "There's nothing wrong with poetry. Sometimes it's the only way you can sort out your thoughts and say what's in your heart. And don't give up. Somebody'll come along—some drifter who'll give you a hand. Maybe he'll even have gumption enough to stick around in spite of Madison until you've got your ranch back in shape again."

"I'd like to think so—"

"Pete Lynch stayed on. Maybe he wasn't a top hand but seems he was willing—and Madison and his bunch didn't scare him off. There are plenty of men like that— ones that don't scare easy. I expect there'll be a couple drop by here right about when you're needing them most. Things just kind of work out that way."

Hetty Judson sighed and got to her feet. "I hope you're right, Mr. Rutledge," she said, and then smiled at him as he drew his lank shape upright. "I want to thank you for what you've done."

"No need. Was glad to help."

"It's late now," she continued as she collected the two spades. "I want you to stay for supper. At least let me show you my appreciation that much."

John Rutledge glanced to the sun. The afternoon was well on its way to evening. He hadn't noticed how time had passed.

"It will be my pleasure," he said politely, crossing to the horses.

7

To John Rutledge's thinking the supper was a fine one—
steak, fried potatoes, milk gravy, hot biscuits, honey, and
good, strong coffee—but Hetty apologized for it. She declared that it had been little more than a spur-of-the-
moment affair and if she'd been given more time she
could have done right, as she expressed it, by their first
and only guest in years.

Rutledge, seated on the porch that ran the width of the
house, was enjoying the evening. Earlier, while turning
his horse into the corral nearby, he had treated himself to
a drink from his bottle, and now, with a full belly, a cigar
clamped between his teeth, and comfortably settled in a
cowhide rocker, he was taking his ease in the warm hush.

From the edge of the porch Willa studied him covertly.
Once he caught her glance, winked, and smiled, but she
instantly turned from him. Inside the house Hetty was restoring the kitchen to its usual arrangement. She was
humming softly, and Rutledge could see her through the
window that opened out onto the porch as she moved
back and forth—beautiful, efficient, and resolute.

"Hypatia," he said, voicing a thought. "Hypatia of the
frontier."

Willa frowned, overhearing. "That's not my mama's
name."

Rutledge removed the cigar from his teeth. "I know, but she reminds me of her."

"Was that her name?"

"It was. I read about her in a book. She was very beautiful and wise. Could do anything she wanted."

"Did she live around here?" Willa asked, warming slightly to him.

"No, in a land called Egypt—a long ways from here."

"I know about Egypt," Willa said at once. "Mama used to read about it to me from my Bible story book."

Rutledge nodded. "A lot of things happened there—good things."

"And bad ones, too—"

"For certain," Rutledge agreed. "That's the way it is everywhere—all over the world in fact—I'm afraid. There's always bad with good."

"This sounds like a serious conversation," Hetty observed, coming through the doorway and out onto the porch.

Earlier she had changed her rough work clothing for a dress and had arranged her hair, piling it on top of her head in a sort of coil. Her face was a bit flushed from the heat of the kitchen stove, which served to deepen the blue of her eyes.

"Very serious," Rutledge replied, rising from his chair at her approach. She smiled, waved him back, and sat down in the other rocker.

"He said you make him think of another lady," Willa volunteered. "Her name is Hy—Hypat—"

"Never mind," Rutledge cut in gently. "I'm sure your mama's not interested in my comments."

Hetty smoothed the folds in the lap of her dress. "Perhaps, but I am interested in offering you a job," she said.

"There's no point in telling you what you'd be taking on—that it not only would be hard work but dangerous as well. You've seen that at first hand."

She hesitated, considered him speculatively. He had tipped back his head and was blowing trembling smoke rings into the motionless air while Willa, fascinated, watched. The last of the sun's light was a coral flare in the western sky and his features, catching the reflection, took on a bronzed, chiseled look.

"I figure you're one man who can handle Cain Madison and that bunch of hard cases who work for him. And that's what I'm looking for, a real man who—"

She stopped short as he lowered his head and faced her directly. Smiling in his remote, lonely way, he said, "I'm sorry, Mrs. Judson, but I'm not hunting a job."

Hetty toyed with the fringe of lace on her apron. "I see —but I just wanted you to know that you have a job here if you're of a mind to take it."

"I appreciate that. I'm just riding through—on my way to New Mexico."

"I think I understand," the woman said after a time. Her voice was worn, reflecting the disappointment that she felt. "You're not really a cowhand—and you don't like that kind of work."

"I've done my share of it—"

"But you've had enough—"

Rutledge shrugged. "Man does what he has to sometimes. Day could come when I'll have to nurse cows again."

"You're praying that it never will."

"Praying's maybe not the right word, but it's close," he said with a grin and threw a glance to the west. The sun

was gone and only a faint reddish glare marked the point
of its disappearance. "Time I was riding on."

"Riding on!" Hetty echoed in a falling voice.

"Yeh, my favorite part of the day to be traveling. The
heat's gone, it's quiet, and everything's sort of going to
rest. A man can get a lot of serious thinking done."

Hetty shook her head. "No—I won't hear of it! You'll
stay here the night. There's a good bunkhouse back there
where you can sleep. And in the morning I'll fix you a big
breakfast that'll carry you clear through the day."

"Seems a powerful lot of trouble for you—"

"It's the kind I enjoy," Hetty said at once. "Now, how
about a little dessert—pie and coffee? It's dried peach
but—"

"Sounds fine to me," Rutledge said, rocking forward in
his chair with the intention of following her into the
kitchen. She waved him back.

"Stay right where you are. We'll have it in high style—
out here on what we, back home, would call the veranda.
Come on Willa, you can help me serve."

Hetty stood in the warm shadows on the porch and
watched John Rutledge go about the task of unsaddling
his horse in the corral. Earlier he had brought up a forkful
of fresh hay and a half a bucket of oats from the barn for
the big sorrel and then, after he had finally accepted her
suggestion to spend the night, had taken his leave and
gone to get the horse set for the night.

Now, the chore finished, he had slung his saddlebags
over a shoulder and was walking briskly toward the bunkhouse, the rhythmic beat of his boot heels a hollow sound
in the quiet.

He was a strange man. Hetty had recognized that fact

almost at once. Quiet, almost deadly in manner, with a tinge of bitterness not only in his eyes but in his voice, he undoubtedly was far above the average in background and education, and had pleased Willa, who came out of her shell somewhat, with a tale of a captive princess and a knight in gleaming armor.

His comparison of her to Hypatia had flattered and startled her. Egypt's legendary paragon of womanhood had long since retreated from memory and to have her brought to mind by a man she had assumed to have firsthand acquaintance with matters pertaining only to the roughshod country in which he lived had been a surprise. Willa, of course, had understood but little of that, but the name had intrigued her and she had repeated it over and over as she went about making herself ready for bed.

John Rutledge fascinated the child, Hetty realized, and then, motionless there in the night, eyes fixed on the door of the bunkhouse beyond which he had disappeared, she admitted to herself that he had the same effect upon her.

She wondered if there was anything to be gained by repeating her offer of a job, perhaps making it more attractive by increasing the amount of pay? Or why not propose a partnership, a three-way arrangement involving him, Willa, and herself? She had never once considered surrendering any part of the ranch to anyone, having sworn at the time of her husband's death to hold onto the place at all costs for Willa's sake. But this would be different. She and Willa would still own most of the ranch —two thirds, in fact—and it would not be the same as selling out, or giving up.

But even as she rolled the idea about in her mind, she had deep-seated feelings that it was a futile hope. Rutledge was not a man to tie himself down. He was a free spirit, one that could be likened to the great, golden-winged eagles that soared high overhead. He might pause to rest, as did they, but never for long. For him there was too much to be seen on the yonder side of the hill, or the flat that stretched, endless, before him.

But, it wouldn't hurt to ask, to broach the proposition of a partnership. Hetty studied the yellow lamplight filling the bunkhouse window with thoughtful eyes for a long minute and then, coming to a decision, wheeled and entered the house. Going to a closet, she withdrew a blanket, tucking it under an arm, and stepped out into the soft night making her way to his quarters.

She halted outside the door, the odor of his cigar meeting her head on. A moment of indecision struck her but she shrugged it off and, raising a hand, knocked firmly on the thick panel. Again uncertainty gripped her. She had the feeling that she could be intruding and the impulse to turn away was strong. But the fear vanished abruptly as the door swung inward and Rutledge stood framed in the opening.

He had removed his boots and shirt, wore only pants, underclothes and socks. His skin below the line of his collar was cotton white and contrasted sharply with that exposed to the sun, which was a deep brown. He held a book in one hand, a finger inserted to retain the page where he had been reading. The cigar between his teeth was freshly lit, and on a table next to the bunk he had chosen she could see a bottle of whiskey along with the lamp and several more books.

There was both question and amusement in his manner as he smiled at her, and Hetty, feeling like a schoolgirl, hastened to explain.

"I thought you might need an extra blanket. It gets right cool here early in the morning."

"I'm obliged to you, Mrs. Judson," he said and stepped back. "Won't you come in?"

"Only for a minute," she replied without hesitation and, entering, moved by him. Dropping the blanket on one of the unused bunks, she turned to him. "I see you like to read. What—"

He raised the book he was holding that she might see its cover. "Shakespeare," he said.

"And these?" she continued, crossing to the table. She was being shamelessly inquisitive, Hetty knew, but John Rutledge now piqued her interest to the point of distraction. Halting, she picked up several of the small, pocket-size volumes.

"Plutarch's *Lives*," she murmured, reading aloud. "Donne, the *Rubaiyat*, Macaulay, *Ancient Rome*, John Milton—oh, Milton! He's my favorite poet." She pivoted, faced him. "You certainly are surprising, Mr. Rutledge."

He shrugged. While she had been perusing his books he had pulled on his shirt and now stood before her more suitably dressed. "It's the one link I have with the past that I've never cared to break," he said. Then he added, faint amusement in his tone, "You seem surprised to find someone out here familiar with the classics."

"Frankly, I am. You're the very first. I haven't laid eyes on books like these since I left home—upstate New York— a hundred years ago it seems." Hetty's voice had become pensive. Opening the thin volume of Milton, she began to leaf through its crisp pages. "'L'Allegro'—I've always loved that poem."

"It's a favorite of mine, too," Rutledge said, striking a match to the tip of his cigar, renewing its life. "Would

you do the honors? I've found poetry is best when someone else reads it aloud to you. The meaning seems to
come through clearer."

Hetty bit at her lower lip in hesitation, glanced at him.
"I don't know—it's late—"

Rutledge smiled. In the glow of the lamp's light, he appeared taller and his eyes were like sharp points.

"On the contrary, Mrs. Judson, it's early. I'll take the
chair, you sit on the edge of the bed where the light is
best. I think this will turn out to be a most enjoyable evening for us both."

Hetty's lips parted as they formed a word of assent. It
would be a treat, all right, spending a few hours with a
man who was familiar with the old masters of words and
with whom she could converse freely about them. Hesitating no longer, she moved to the bunk and sat down.

8

The sudden rattle of gunshots and the thud of running horses brought John Rutledge out of his bunk in a plunging leap. He had reacted instantly to the sounds just as he now automatically snatched one of the pistols hanging in its holster from the back of a chair and rushed to the door.

He had been asleep for a bit more than three hours, having turned out the lamp and crawled in between his blankets shortly after Hetty Judson had departed. They had enjoyed the time spent together, reading passages from his books and discussing many things that they discovered interested them both.

Pulling the door open a narrow crack, Rutledge glanced out. The moon and stars were bright and he had no trouble seeing the half a dozen or so riders wheeling in and out of the yard, all firing indiscriminately at whatever caught their attention.

They were Madison riders he saw moments later when one of them swept in close. The rancher's Circle M brand —the same mark he'd noted at the time Pete Lynch was executed—was clearly visible on the horse's hip. Anger tightened Rutledge's mouth and, bringing up his pistol, he snapped a quick shot at the puncher. At that instant the horse veered sharply to avoid the water trough placed a few strides out in front of the bunkhouse, and the bullet went wide.

Immediately a hail of lead struck the front of the structure, some of it slamming into the door itself, other slugs hammering into the plank wall and shattering the glass in the window. Grim, swearing deeply, Rutledge jerked back. Pivoting, he returned to his bunk, pulled on his clothes, and strapping on his guns, crossed to the other door at the back of the bunkhouse, yanked it open, and stepped out into the night.

He could not see the Circle M riders from there but the sound of their yells and gunshots and the pound of their horses' hoofs filled the warm air. And there was something else: the lurid glow of fire was now beginning to light up the area.

Anxious, fearing for Hetty and her small daughter, Rutledge hurriedly circled the squat bunkhouse and came to the yard. Roaring flames were consuming a small shed about halfway between him and the main house. Another fire had been started in the dry weeds near the barn. Suddenly, one of Madison's riders, a blazing torch in his upraised hand, rode in close to the ranch house and tossed the burning faggot against the south wall of the structure.

Rutledge shouted and, both guns drawn, began to run toward the house. Hetty and Willa would be trapped if they were inside, and likely they were. They would have been afraid to come out while the Circle M riders continued to race about, shooting recklessly.

Rutledge slowed. The air was heavy with dust and smoke and sharp with the odor of burnt gunpowder, and it was difficult to see for any distance. Abruptly, a rider whipped by him. The man, surprised by his appearance, rocked to one side of his saddle, and triggered a quick shot.

John, moving on, threw an answering bullet at the cow-hand's retreating shape. The man winced, and suddenly rigid in the saddle, let his arms drop to his sides, swerved, and raced away. Others swung in behind him, bursting out of the pall where they had been invisible, and shortly there were only the flat echoes of their galloping horses as they vanished into the night.

Slipping his pistols back into their holsters, Rutledge wheeled, grabbing up an empty feed sack lying near the water trough. Quickly soaking it, he ran to the wall of the house where flames, having ignited the sun-dried wood, were beginning to climb. Reaching the structure, he began to beat at the darting tongues with the dripping sack.

At that moment he saw Hetty, followed by her small daughter, come from the rear of the building. The woman had caught up another sack, wet it, and was hurrying to help while Willa, apparently having received instructions from her mother, began to work the hand pump and refill the trough.

Shoulder to shoulder, Rutledge and Hetty slashed and beat at the stubborn flames, returning several times to the trough to soak their sacks. Finally the fire at that point was out. Immediately Rutledge turned and started to-ward the shed. It was by then a mass of flames.

"No use," Hetty called to him above the crackling. "We can't stop it now. It was empty, anyway."

She was breathing hard from her efforts, as was Rut-ledge, and both turned their attention then to the fire near the barn. It was all but out of its own accord. Flames had eaten through the dry weeds and grass, reached a barren strip, and there, short of the structure, died off.

Rutledge threw his sack aside, glanced at Hetty. Soot streaked his face and blackened his hands and arms, and there were several small, still smoking holes in his shirt where live coals had fallen. Pinching out the last of them, he said, "Glad you and the little girl weren't hurt."

Hetty brushed at her forehead with the back of a hand. There were smudges of black on her skin, too, and the light robe she had hastily donned over her nightgown also bore the scars of fire.

"We stayed down close to the floor," she replied, wearily.

"There much damage?"

"The windows—they shot out all of them. And one of them threw a rope about the hitch rack, dragged it off. I—I don't know of anything else except the fires, of course."

Hetty paused, smiled up at him as Willa moved in close and caught her hand. "I have to thank you again. Your coming out when you did stopped them. I shudder to think what they would have done if you hadn't been here."

"Expect that was sort of a surprise," Rutledge said. "They got rid of Pete Lynch, figured that left you and the little girl here alone." He paused and shook his head slowly. Voice hardening, he added, "The kind of men who show up in the middle of the night to make war on a lone woman sure don't count for much."

"That's Cain Madison's way of doing things. You saw for certain that it was his bunch, didn't you?"

Rutledge nodded but his glance had drifted to the corral where he had put his horse for the night. Abruptly he moved off and in long, quick strides crossed the smoke-filled yard to the gate of the enclosure. A low curse came from his lips.

"What is it?" Hetty asked, coming up to him. She was alone, having sent Willa back to the house.

For an answer he pointed into the shadowy depths of the corral. The big sorrel lay flat on the ground, two legs doubled beneath him, two stiffly extended, the head oddly twisted to one side.

"They—they killed him!"

Rutledge made no reply. Opening the gate, he stepped inside the small fenced yard and moved to where the animal lay. Kneeling beside him, he made his examination. After a time he rose and returned to the gate. His jaw was set and his eyes looked small and hard as agate.

"Not an accident—not a stray bullet," he said, closing the gate and rejoining the woman. "Was shot four times. They did it just for the hell of doing it."

A sound of disgust escaped Hetty's throat. "That's the first horse they've shot. There's been steers, and our dogs, but they've let the horses be."

"Usually how it is—no matter what the trouble is about," Rutledge said. "It's sort of understood that you don't kill a horse. I've run up against some mighty small men in my time, but this Cain Madison's looking like he might take the prize."

"He's the worst kind," Hetty stated flatly. "Believe me, I know from first hand! And the men who work for him are just like him. It's as if they've been infected by his poison. Some of them do things I'm certain they wouldn't ordinarily do."

"Like shooting a horse penned up in a corral," Rutledge said, his voice low and taut.

"That's just what I mean. I—I feel responsible for this, John. I want you to pick yourself a horse from my string. I don't have many—six or seven that are good saddle stock, but you're welcome to any of them."

Rutledge half turned, raised his head, and stared off into the night. The planes of his face were flat and shone dully in the pale light.

"Obliged, but it's not up to you," he said, finally. "It's between me and Madison."

Hetty frowned, started to speak, but hesitated as Willa came running up with a shawl in her hands. Taking the garment from her daughter, the woman draped it about her shoulders, shivering a bit from the night's coolness as she did so.

"I don't understand," she said, then. "Why Madison?"

"His hired hands were the ones who killed my horse—and that makes him the one who owes me. If you'll loan me something to ride I'll go over to his place in the morning and do some collecting."

Hetty Judson was looking at him, a mixture of admiration and incredulity in her eyes. "You're going to confront Cain Madison in his own yard and demand that he give—replace your horse?"

"He's the one responsible."

"But to go there, just ride right into his place—it'll be too risky!"

Rutledge shrugged and looked down at Willa, pressing close to her mother's side. "Most everything a man does nowadays is risky. Anyway, there's the little matter of me being in the right and him in the wrong."

A wide smile was on Hetty Judson's lips. "Do you mind if I tag along with you? I want to see the look on Cain Madison's face when you collar him."

Rutledge gave that thought. "Could be risky, like you say—but it's up to you," he replied after a time.

Hetty shook her head. "I've got a feeling that all of the risk's going to be on Madison's part," she said, and smiled again.

9

Early that following morning, Rutledge hitched two of Hetty Judson's work horses to a chain pull and, attaching it to the luckless sorrel, dragged the carcass off into a deep arroyo west of the ranch house. There, with the aid of a spade, he caved in the sides of the wash and effectively covered over the dead gelding.

By the time he had finished and was back in the barn, Hetty had breakfast prepared and was calling to him. He washed up and reported to the kitchen where he ate quickly. Within the hour they were en route to Madison's Circle M ranch. Hetty, astride her bay mare, guided him across the short hills and flats on a direct course.

Rutledge, features set to their usual somber lines, had taken a drink from his bottle just before mounting the black lent him by Hetty, and as they rode through the midmorning freshness he maintained the silence she had come to associate with him. He was, she had learned, even in an acquaintance so short, a man of many moods. He could be either talkative and congenial, morose and tight-lipped, or angrily sullen—all depending upon the circumstances. But, regardless of the situation, she found him always polite and courteous and unfailingly considerate.

"Not too sure your coming along was a smart idea," he

said, breaking his stillness as they pulled to a halt outside the high, pole gate fronting Madison's place.

"Why not?" she countered. "I'm mixed up in this as much as you. Besides, you didn't know the way here."

"Expect I could've found it," he said dryly and looked directly at her. His eyes had hardened to small, colorless points and the set of his features combined to give him an unforgiving, lethal sort of appearance. "Keep out of the way—that clear?"

"Clear," Hetty murmured, subdued by the sheer violence that she now recognized in him.

Rutledge nodded brusquely, and brushing the butts of the pistols at his sides with the palms of his hands, he clucked softly to his horse and turned into the lane leading to the house.

It was a fine, well-kept place. There were no aging, weathered structures in need of repair to be seen. The corral poles were neatly whitewashed, and the main house was trim and solid-looking and apparently had recently been repainted. The ranch had the appearance of being strictly business with no time or effort wasted on frills.

"Has Madison got a wife?" Rutledge asked as they pulled up in front of the house. The yard was deserted except for a man forking manure onto a flat-bed wagon standing near a barn.

"No, he's a widower. I guess she died—or maybe left him—before he came here. He has a son—Clint. He's about twenty or so and—"

"Who keeps house for him?"

"I don't know. I think somebody said he had a Mexican woman."

"It sure is lonesome," Rutledge said, his glance continuing restlessly to probe the yard and its structures.

"That's what you can expect from Madison. He'll have everybody that works for him off doing something."

Rutledge's shoulders stirred. "I came to talk," he said and, drawing one of his pistols, drove a bullet through the dormer window in the slanting roof of the house.

A yell sounded from somewhere inside the structure, and back at the crew's quarters—a low, rambling building standing midway between the principal house and the barn—two men abruptly appeared. Their movements caught Rutledge's eye.

"Who're they?"

Hetty swept the pair with a quick look. "The tall one's Dave Hollander—Madison's foreman. I don't know the name of the other. There's Cain Madison now—"

Rutledge had seen the rancher at that same moment. He had come from the side of the house as if fearing to use the front door placed in the exact center of the wall and of the porch that ran the full width of the building.

"Stay clear of me," Rutledge warned again, still holding the pistol with which he had shattered the window glass in his hand.

The rancher was a big man, tall with weight to go with his height. Perhaps fifty, he had a round, ruddy face, hard, small dark eyes and a thin mouth with a gray downcurving mustache. He was well dressed: creased, tan corduroy pants, white shirt gartered at the elbows, black string tie, and polished boots. He wore no hat at that moment, and was also unarmed. Stepping up onto his porch, he folded his arms across his chest and, ignoring Hetty Judson, glared at Rutledge.

"Who the hell are you and what do you mean shooting

out my window?" he demanded angrily. "I'll have you—"

"Name's Rutledge. You owe me a horse and this lady—"

"Owe you a horse—the hell I do! What gives you that idea?"

Rutledge's glance was also on Hollander and the cowhand, who were hurriedly approaching from the bunkhouse. So far he could not see that the gunshot had attracted any more Circle M hired help except them. Nevertheless, he was taking no chances and, kneeing his mount slightly about, he placed his back to a close-by windbreak of dense salt cedars.

"Your bunch of *bravos* rode into this lady's ranch last night and shot it up. Did some burning—and they killed my horse. Were four bullets in him, so don't tell me it was an accident."

Madison's attitude changed. He drew himself up arrogantly. "So? What about it? Your own damn fault if you got caught hanging around that—"

Rutledge moved slightly as he triggered the weapon in his hand for a second time. Splinters and a puff of dust flew from the plank floor at the rancher's feet.

Cain Madison yelled and jumped back. He threw a hurried glance at Hollander and the man with him, now at the opposite end of the porch.

Rutledge's narrowed eyes were on them also. "Can stop right there," he called softly.

The ranch foreman and the cowhand pulled up short, the latter making a remark of some sort to his companion.

Rutledge shook his head. "Best you keep out of this," he warned. "It's between him and me. You try taking a hand and I'll kill." His voice, at the last, was low, cold as winter's wind, and left no room for doubt.

Madison, his features an angry red, was cursing steadily. He pointed a long finger at Hollander. "Speak up, Dave! What's this all about? He telling me for true about his damned horse and the woman's place?"

Hollander nodded. "Some of the boys rode over there last night, all right. That's where Lon Tyler got that bullet in his arm. I didn't know about the drifter's horse, however."

"He was a good animal," Rutledge said, the pistol now leveled idly at Madison. "Stood around fifteen hands, was three years old. I want one to match him."

"You can go straight to hell!" the rancher shouted. "I ain't about to give—"

"Maybe we better do what he says, Mr. Madison," Hollander, eyes on Rutledge, cut in. "It was our boys that done it."

"How the hell do you know it was them that shot down his damned horse? Who's to say that he—"

"You calling me a liar?" Rutledge asked in a soft, pressing way.

Madison frowned. Although the morning was still cool, sweat had gathered on his forehead. Reaching up, he nervously wiped it away.

"Well, it's only that I ain't exactly for sure about this," he said hesitantly.

"Your outfit killed him—put four bullets in him just as I've said. And while we're talking about the damage your bunch did hurrahing the place, you owe the lady for a dozen window glasses they shot out and a shed they set fire to."

Cain Madison's color deepened as rage swept through him. "By God—that's enough! I ain't doing—"

"He's right, Mr. Madison," Hollander interrupted once again. "The boys did tear up the place considerable. I reckon we do owe Mrs. Judson. Expect we can settle with her for a couple of double eagles. And that black gelding with the white stockings, he'll do to give Rutledge."

Madison was rubbing at his chin in agitation. "Just who the hell you working for, Dave?" he demanded.

Hollander returned the rancher's stare. "I'm doing what I know's best," he replied. "I'm looking out for you."

Madison remained silent for a long breath, and then shrugged. "All right," he said. "Give him the black."

"I'll take a bill of sale with your name on it, too, Madison," Rutledge said.

The rancher only nodded. Hollander turned and said something to the man with him, who wheeled and trotted off toward a row of corrals at the lower end of the yard.

"I'll get the papers," Hollander said then and, moving by Madison, stepped up onto the porch and disappeared into the house.

Rutledge, his eyes continually roving the yard for signs of the rancher's hired hands, should they put in an appearance, let them pause on Hetty.

"Two double eagles—that be enough to pay for the damage they did to your place?"

She nodded and held her place a bit to the side of him where she would not be in the line of fire if trouble arose. "This time, anyway."

"There something else that needs settling up?"

Hetty gave that thought, shook her head. "No, it's done and gone. And for what he did to Jack—he hasn't got enough money to ever pay for that—for his life."

A twisted smile pulled at John Rutledge's mouth. "No? Well, maybe you'd like his life in pay for your husband's. It won't take but one bullet—"

Madison dropped back a step, fear tearing at his face.

He looked wildly about for help but there was none to be seen.

Hetty frowned and shook her head quickly. "No, I'd not want that—not cold-blooded murder—"

The crooked smile was still on Rutledge's mouth. "That's the trouble with you God-fearing people—you're too soft-hearted. Makes it easy for his kind to stomp on you."

"Maybe, but I won't stoop to murder."

Rutledge shrugged and settled his full attention on Madison. "You remember this—you owe this lady your life. I'd as soon kill you as not for what you've done to her, but she says no."

Cain Madison, thoroughly cowed, again rubbed nervously at his jaw. "I never meant to—"

"The hell you didn't!" Rutledge snapped, cutting off whatever it was the rancher intended to deny. "You bushwhacked her husband, or had one of your hired hands do it. Maybe she can't prove it but we all know it's true. And you've been hurrahing her ever since, trying to make her sell out to you. She tells me she won't—that she doesn't intend to, ever. Now, mister, you take that as your answer once and for all and leave her alone? Understand?"

The rancher looked away. "Understand," he mumbled.

The man who had gone for the replacement horse appeared, leading a tall black with four white-stockinged legs up from a corral. At the same moment, Hollander came through the doorway of the house, a square of paper and a pen and bottle of ink in his hands. The arrival of the two men seemed to strengthen Cain Madison's backbone.

"You talk mighty big with that hog leg in your hand,"

he said. "You can see I ain't armed—and that all my hired help's off working 'cept for Hollander and Payson, here."

"No problem," Rutledge drawled. "Be pleased to wait while you get your gun."

Madison turned to Hollander and slowly scribbled his signature on the bill of sale, apparently taking it as an opportunity to ignore Rutledge's suggestion. Finished, he returned the paper to his foreman who came down off the porch and crossed to where Rutledge sat slackly in his saddle.

"He's a good horse," he said, handing the papers to the tall rider. "Sound, plenty of bottom. I know because I've rode him some myself."

"I'll take your word for it," Rutledge responded coolly. "If you've suckered me, I'll be back." Abruptly, he shifted his attention to Madison. "We'll take that pay for the damages your bunch did. Three double eagles'll cover it."

Madison dug into his pocket, paused. "Two—that's what we said."

"Three's what I'm saying," Rutledge stated coldly. "The lady's being generous with you again."

Cain Madison swore raggedly, selected the specified amount from the handful of coins he produced from a leather poke, and flipped them to Hollander. The foreman neatly caught the gold pieces and relayed them to Rutledge.

Passing the money on to Hetty, Rutledge holstered his pistol and accepted the black's lead rope from the man called Payson.

"Like to tell you one more thing," he said, attaching the rope to a ring in his saddle skirt. "I don't want you or any of your outfit trailing us after we ride out of here. You send somebody, I'll kill them. Hear?"

Madison made no immediate reply; he simply stood quietly and accepted the cold, matter-of-fact words of warning. Then he stirred. "Yeh, I hear, but I reckon you wouldn't be so damn high and mighty if some of my hired hands was around—somebody like Ed Drace."

Rutledge cut his horse about, motioning at Hetty to pull out. "Doubt if it'd make any difference," he said, swinging in behind the woman. He let his flat eyes halt on Payson and Dave Hollander. "Don't go trying to be heroes. What I said goes for you, too."

10

As they drew near the gate Hetty Judson turned, looked back. She was not at all convinced that Cain Madison would heed Rutledge's warning; his soaring, unbridled pride would never permit it. The rancher had not moved, however, and was at that moment standing just where he had been, talking to Dave Hollander and the other ranch hand who had been present—Payson, or whatever his name was. That Cain was furious was easily recognizable in the gestures he was making and the high color of his features.

"Something bothering you?"

At Rutledge's question, Hetty shifted her attention to him. "Just wanted to see what Madison is doing. He'll never let you get away with what you did to him without striking back. I guess you know that."

"Yeh, reckon I do. Always makes me feel good, though, to take his kind down a few notches."

Hetty smiled. "You certainly did that, making him give you a horse and me the money to cover my broken windows."

"Who's Ed Drace? Seems mighty proud of him." They had reached the gate and were moving into the low hills that lay between the Circle M and the Judson place.

"A hired gunman. He is the one who did all the hard work—the persuading—for Madison when he was buying up ranches around here and ran into somebody who wouldn't sell out."

Rutledge nodded. "Can expect to hear from him then, I reckon."

"No doubt. And from Clint Madison, too. He fancies himself a real hard case, just like Drace. Patterns himself after him. Can bet he'll be looking for you after the way you humbled his pa."

Rutledge shrugged. "Seems I've done some stirring in a hornet's nest. What about Hollander? I'd pick him to be a square shooter."

"Far as I know, he is. Never could understand why he stayed on with Madison. He was foreman on the ranch when Cain bought it." She paused, laughed. "He came to see me not long after Jack was killed. I don't know if Madison sent him or not, but he told me in a nice way that I ought to sell out for my own sake—that there was a lot more to running a ranch than wearing a man's pants and shirt, and being able to shoot."

"The man could've meant it—could've wanted to spare you a lot of trouble."

"I've thought of that," Hetty admitted, "and maybe it's true. But it didn't change my mind any."

Rutledge made no comment as they rode slowly on. The sand hills were behind them now and they were coming into the band of trees and brush that lay like a ragged green ribbon across that part of the country.

A feeling of apprehension began to grow within Hetty, and as they came to the first of the brake, she again twisted about on her saddle and looked back. There was no one in sight. She sighed, relieved, and glanced at Rutledge, now riding abreast and a bit to the right of her. He appeared cool, calm, utterly unconcerned with the possibility that there might be some of Cain Madison's men following them.

She supposed it didn't really matter to him. That he was, himself, a gunman of considerable ability had become evident, just as it was plain that he had no conception of fear. Further, she could see that it mattered little to him what the outcome of any incident, such as she'd just witnessed, might be. He was a man with little regard for life, his or others—a quality that she supposed stemmed from the bitterness that lay within him, which, in turn, had its roots in the past. What it all amounted to, Hetty decided, was a definite death wish.

She could never have imagined a man being so cool as he had been when he summoned the all-powerful Cain Madison by the direct and forceful method of shooting out one of his windows. He could not have known that most of the rancher's hired hands—the bully boys—would be away at that time, thus it had not mattered to him whether they were absent or not. The fact that he would have faced overwhelming odds had they been there apparently did not enter his mind.

And when they had taken their leave—after he'd forced Madison to accede to his demands—he had not merely voiced a threat relative to Circle M riders' giving pursuit, he had made a flat statement. And the manner in which he had said it should have left no doubt in the minds of all who heard it that he meant every word. It was more like a promise.

"Keep riding."

Rutledge's voice broke into Hetty's thoughts. She turned to him as he spoke again. "Be obliged if you'll take my horse with you."

He was looking back over the trail that cut through the

trees and brush. Turning her attention to that direction, Hetty too caught sight of the three riders coming on at a fast lope. She studied them closely and recognized one as Clint Madison. The others were nameless hired hands.

She slowed her horse to keep alongside Rutledge, shaking her head. He gave her a direct, expressionless look and passed the black's lead rope to her.

"Go," he said bluntly. "I don't want you around where you might get hurt. I'll meet you at your house soon as I take care of this bit of business."

He swerved away immediately after that and rode a short distance back along the trail and halted, this time stopping in its center to block the oncoming riders' passage. Hetty, stubbornly determined not to be left out, continued for a few yards and pulled off into the brush. Although she had supreme confidence in John Rutledge, she felt he just might need a little help; after all, the odds would be three to his one.

"Close enough!"

Hetty heard Rutledge call out his warning and saw Clint Madison and the two men with him round a slight bend in the trail some thirty or forty feet away.

"I'll say when I'm close enough!" the younger Madison yelled back. His face was stiff with anger. Evidently he had arrived at the ranch only minutes after she and Rutledge had ridden out. Learning what had taken place, he had called on a couple of the Circle M men to side him and had set out to right what he considered a blight on the family honor.

"If you're wanting to die, come six foot nearer," Rutledge said quietly.

She could not see his features but his eyes would have squeezed down to narrow slits and there would be that small, mocking half smile on his lips—just as she had seen him when he faced Cain Madison.

Clint slowed, then drew to a stop. The two riders, one on either side, halted also.

"I don't know who the hell you figure you are," Clint began, his voice trembling with rage, "but you ain't getting away with what you done—riding in, shooting up the place, ragging my pa like you did!"

"Go on home, boy," Rutledge replied softly.

"You ain't dealing with no old man who didn't have a gun on him," Clint continued, his voice lifting. "You're up against somebody that ain't going to back off!"

"Go on home," Rutledge repeated in the same, unhurried way. "I don't want to kill you."

"Kill *me!*" Clint shouted. "You ain't about to! You maybe bamboozled Hollander and that other jasper, but you ain't me!"

John Rutledge shifted on his saddle, the movement slight but enough to set him square in the hull and place his pistols within quick reach.

"You think you can take me, boy?" he asked, putting emphasis on the last word. "If you do, you're fooling yourself even with your two friends there to help. I'll tell you plain, you'll never make it."

Clint Madison glanced at his friends and snorted. "You sure got a mighty good opinion of yourself, drifter!"

"Comes from knowing what you can do," Rutledge said. "Now turn around and head back to your pa. We had an understanding about bothering me and Mrs. Judson and I don't figure he'd want you going against it."

"That's a damn lie!" Clint shouted. "Pa never made you no deal like that!"

Rutledge stiffened slightly. "Best you trot back to your

house and ask him," he said. "He knows what'll happen if he ever again bothers the lady."

The younger Madison leaned forward, a scornful expression on his face. "And just what do you reckon that'd be? You going to come over and shoot out some more of our windows?"

"No, I'll kill him—and anybody else that gets in my way," Rutledge replied evenly.

"You—you won't do nothing!" Clint yelled abruptly and made a stab for the pistol on his hip. "Shoot him!"

Hetty saw Rutledge's shoulders dip forward briefly. In that same fragment of time both of his guns fired. Clint Madison rocked back on his saddle and began to fall. One of the two men with him, horse shying wildly, was also reeling. The other, both hands raised above his head, was shouting loudly through the floating smoke streamers that he wanted no part of the shoot-out.

Hetty shivered. The deadliness, the precision, and the calm efficiency with which Rutledge shot Clint Madison and his friend filled her with a sort of chilling admiration and respect. Straining to hear better, she moved closer to the trail.

The rider who had indicated his unwillingness to draw his weapon was looking questioningly at Rutledge, as if seeking permission to dismount. Rutledge nodded slightly and the man came off his horse, dropped to his knees beside the sprawling figure of the rancher's son. After a moment he glanced up.

"Dead. You got him through the heart."

Rutledge was motionless for a breath or two, as if not hearing, and then his shoulders stirred. Rocking back, he holstered one of his pistols.

"Was him that wanted this, not me," he said.

"Maybe so," the puncher said, rising, "but that ain't going to cut no hay with his pa. You've gone and killed Cain Madison's boy and he'll be coming to make you pay for doing it."

Rutledge shrugged again. "He knows where to find me," he said, and added, "He send the boy out on my trail?"

"Nope, he didn't. Clint just took off with me and Amos there, after he heard what you'd done. He never talked with the old man."

"Expect he should have," Rutledge said mildly and glanced at the other cowhand, slumped in his saddle and clutching at his side. "Better get your friend there to the doc. He's bleeding bad. One thing, I'll be expecting you to tell Madison the truth about what happened here."

The rider standing over Clint's body nodded slowly. "Only right that I do, but I don't figure it'll make no difference. Way I see it, you're dead as Clint there, only it ain't happened yet."

"Could be," Hetty heard Rutledge say as he swung about and headed back up the trail.

11

With the grim, hard-set lines of his features fading, John Rutledge continued along the trail. He had not wanted trouble with Cain Madison's son—little more than a boy in years—and had done his best to avoid it. But, as was his way, he refused to back down from a confrontation, and this one had ended with the usual result.

And this one could have unwanted repercussions, not for him but for Hetty Judson. That realization brought a dark scowl to his face. He should have thought of that and avoided a shoot-out with Clint Madison. Rutledge shrugged off the moment of self-censure; at such times a man was not permitted the luxury of vagrant thoughts— he concentrated strictly on the crisis at hand, else he likely ended up dead.

Motion ahead caught his attention. He glanced up, saw Hetty Judson ride out of the brush shouldering the trail and halt, awaiting him. Rutledge swore quietly. She had witnessed the shooting. He searched her eyes carefully seeking some indication of her reaction. It appeared to be mixed—of relief and anger. A hard smile cracked his lips. Women sure as hell were hard to understand at times.

"Told you to ride on," he said stiffly. He noticed then that her pistol was in her hand. "Now, just what the hell did you figure to do with that?" he added, pointing at the weapon.

Hetty glanced down at the weapon—a nickel-plated, pearl-handled piece of small caliber—probably a thirty-two. Sliding it back into its holster, she said, "I thought you might need help. The odds were bad."

"I'm obliged. . . . Can you hit anything with it?"

"Of course!" Hetty replied. "Jack gave it to me when we first came to this country. I learned to use it, but I'm much better with a rifle."

"Most folks are," Rutledge said absently, glancing back. There was no one on the trail behind them—at least not yet. That would change, however, after the two cowhands reached the Circle M with Clint's body and reported to Cain Madison. The rancher, burning with a desire for vengeance, and with plenty of well-armed help, would come on fast looking for him.

Rutledge gave that realization full consideration. Then, "Been thinking—I'd best be riding on."

They were at that moment crossing a wide, grassy meadow, clean and fresh-smelling in the late morning hours. Hetty swung from her contemplation of it, faced him anxiously.

"Why? Because of what just happened—of Clint Madison?"

He brushed his hat to the back of his head. "That's right. It's going to bring Madison and his gunhands to your place looking for me. If I'm not around, they'll probably leave you be."

"Maybe—anyway, I'm not scared of Madison and what he might do. I've been putting up with him for years. It won't be any different."

"This time it will. His son's dead, and when that happens to a man he goes a little crazy."

"I can look out for myself," Hetty declared stubbornly. "I'm not scared of him—"

"Damn it, woman—you ought to be!" Rutledge snapped, angered by her bland attitude. "A man like Cain Madison won't stop at anything to get his way, or square up for what he figures is a wrong."

Hetty gave him a bitter smile. "Just what do you think I've been doing all this time—since Jack was murdered, in fact? I've been fighting him the best way I can, and I've managed to survive—so don't worry about me, I'll make it." She paused and looked ahead. They had topped out the last low hill and the ranch was in sight. "Still wish you'd go to work for me."

Rutledge shrugged. "That'd bring Madison down on you for sure—"

"Wouldn't make any difference—or change anything, either. And while you're fretting about maybe being the cause of more trouble between Cain Madison and me, and figuring that riding on is the answer, how about looking at it from a different angle?"

"Different?"

"Yes—why not stay around and help me fight him off?"

He grinned at her logic. "I spilled the molasses so ought to help clean it up, that what you mean?"

"Exactly—only I was thinking of it becoming a permanent arrangement. Intended to talk to you about it last night only things got out of hand."

Rutledge, his features drawn into a frown, retrieved his bottle from the saddlebags and helped himself to a generous swallow. Restoring the liquor to its place, he nodded to her.

"Meaning?"

"I was going to offer you a partnership in the ranch. We'd make a good team—"

Rutledge's weather-browned face settled into an expressionless mask. He made no reply and his eyes were partly closed as he stared off into the distance. He was thinking in that moment of another time, of another woman and their partnership—one of marriage. They had been a good team, too, he and Lacey.

"A man is what the ranch needs," Hetty rushed on, mistaking his stony silence for consideration of her proposal. "Lynch, and the others that I've had around, weren't much help—did just what they had to and that halfway most of the time. I know you don't give a rap for being a cowhand. Could tell that from the way you talked about it, but if you were a partner, I thought, maybe you'd see it differently."

They had reached the lane that led to the house and were turning into it. Rutledge lowered his gaze, let it sweep the yard, the buildings, the general area. Everything looked to be as they had left it. He still felt an uneasiness, despite Hetty's assurance, when he thought of her small daughter left there alone.

"What do you think, John? Are you interested in my offer?"

He was an utterly honest man and wasted few words when it was necessary to get to the point. "No," he said. "I'm obliged to you, but it's not my kind of life. I've done my share and I guess you could say that doing it, I got my belly full."

"But just riding—drifting around—that's not a life either."

Rutledge's shoulders moved slightly. They had reached the yard and Willa had come out onto the porch to greet them. She waved to her mother and touched him with a shy glance.

"It's the kind that suits me," he said, answering Hetty's comment. "I like moving on, seeing new country. Somebody once said, there's always something on the yonder side of the next hill that a man ought to have a look at."

"I wonder," Hetty murmured, a tinge of scorn in her tone that revealed the normal distaste of a woman for a man who avoided home ties. "You miss so much—never putting down roots, having a family, building a future for them—for yourself."

"Not saying that doesn't count," Rutledge said quietly. "It did with me, too—once, a long time ago. But that's all over and I've come to look at life a bit different."

They had moved past the house, were pulling up to the first corral—the one in which the sorrel had met his death. Willa, following, was trotting along in their wake.

Hetty sensed immediately the underlying meaning of his dark words. "You don't have to feel that way," she said, swinging off the saddle. "You could find something in this life to live for despite whatever it was in the past that made you change. You don't need to go on looking—well—looking for death."

He gave that thought as he came off his horse and paused beside it. "Not that—I just don't believe in dodging it. If it comes—it comes."

Hetty smiled tightly. "I'm not so sure of that. I think you maybe go out of your way to meet it."

He had followed the horses into the corral and was preparing to strip them of their gear, beginning with her mare.

"Could be," he said in his quiet way, "but if I do, I don't realize it. I figure it's like a friend of mine once told me—every man has a bullet somewhere with his name on it, and he'll live till it comes along."

Hetty shook her head in exasperation. "Where do men get such foolish ideas?" she exclaimed and reached for Willa's hand. And then, blunting this sharpness of her words with a smile, added: "We'll go in and fix some lunch. I'll call you when it's—"

Rutledge had turned away, was looking off to the south of the ranch where a dust cloud was hanging low against the horizon.

"I reckon lunch'll have to wait," he said, his voice quickening almost to a joyous pitch. "Visitors are coming —and they won't be coming friendly."

12

"Madison!" Hetty Judson said as she hurriedly turned her eyes into the direction of the dust.

"Little sooner than I expected," Rutledge said, and taking up the reins of the horse he had been using—still waiting to be unsaddled—led him from the corral into the yard. Halting, the tall rider swung up onto the saddle.

"Want you and the little girl to get inside the house—and stay there," he said crisply.

Hetty shook her head. "No—it's my fight."

"Not this time," he replied. "I'm the one they're looking for. Now do what I say!"

There was no qualification in his voice, no request; it was a hard, direct order. Hetty frowned and bit at her lower lip.

"All right," she said, taking Willa's hand and starting for the house. "Where'll you be?"

"Figuring the size of the party Madison's bringing, I need a bit of an edge. Aim to be waiting for him down by the gate," Rutledge answered and, raking his horse with spurs, raced out of the yard.

He pointed south, that route taking him into a windbreak of tall brush, and, keeping within the ragged bramble so that he would not be seen by the approaching rancher and his men, continued on a course paralleling the lane that led to the house. When he reached the slight bend just beyond the edge of the yard that fronted the Judson ranch house, he stopped.

Rutledge settled back in his saddle and allowed his body to go slack as he drew each of his pistols and checked their cylinders to be certain both were fully loaded. Satisfied they were in their usual smooth working order, he returned them to their well-oiled holsters. Treating himself then to a drink from the bottle in his saddlebags, he folded his arms across his chest and began the wait.

Cain Madison was not long in coming. Rutledge heard the rapid drumming of hoofs, caught the smell of dust in the air, and shortly, through the screen of brush before him, saw the party ride past.

Madison, rigidly upright in his saddle, was slightly ahead of the others. There were eight of them, Rutledge saw, and as he watched, the rancher gave an order of some sort and four of the riders cut away from the lane, two heading into the brush on the left, two doing likewise on the right.

The lines in Rutledge's lean face deepened and a half smile pulled at his mouth. Madison was playing it close to his vest despite the large party he'd brought with him and was taking no chance on coming out second best this time. He'd do his talking from the road while the four men, guns ready, would move in from the sides and neutralize any opposition.

The soft thud of the now-walking horses ceased. Cain had reached the spot where he intended to make his stand—probably at the edge of the yard. From there he would have a clear view of the house, while there would still be heavy brush conveniently nearby into which he

could duck if it became prudent and in which his men
could hide.

With the hard, humorless smile frozen on his lips, Rutledge clucked softly to his horse, left the tangled windbreak, and turning into the lane, rode slowly toward the
house and the line of men, backs to him, facing it. As before, Madison was in the center but the four remaining
riders had pulled abreast and were now at his sides—two
to each shoulder.

"Rutledge!"

At Madison's harsh summons, John Rutledge drew his
pistols and, loose in the saddle, allowed his horse to continue quietly up the lane. When a dozen strides or so yet
remained to separate him from the rancher and his men,
he halted.

"Right here—"

At the unexpected reply Madison and his riders
whirled around. The rancher's small eyes had flared with
surprise, and anger deepened his color.

"And here!"

Hetty Judson's voice carried to them from across the
yard. Rutledge glanced beyond Madison and his party.
Hetty Judson, prone on the roof deck of her house, had a
rifle in her hands and was training it on the rancher. Despite the sudden impatience that swept through him as he
beheld her—deliberately ignoring his instructions to remain inside the house out of harm's way—Rutledge felt a
stir of admiration. Hetty Judson was one hell of a woman!
The smile on his lips widened noticeably.

"You looking for me, Madison?"

The rancher had recovered his aplomb to some extent,
thinking no doubt that while he had been initially out-

maneuvered, the odds were still heavily in his favor, eight to two.

"You're damned right I am!" he shouted. "I've come here to square up!"

"Guess you've got a call to try," Rutledge said coolly. "First you best warn those men you sent off to potshot me from the brush—there's two on my left and two on my right. If any of them makes the slightest sound I'll take it wrong and blow you off your saddle."

Madison shook his head. "You won't hear nothing. I give the sign—you'll be dead."

"Goes for you, too, Madison. I've got my forty-fives lined up on you. A bullet hits me, my trigger fingers shut down—reflex action somebody called it—and the bullets go straight into you. You'll be sliding into hell right alongside of me."

The rancher swore vividly and flung a glance at Hetty Judson on the roof of her house. Rutledge nodded.

"Better not forget her, either. She's up there where she can pick all of you off—one by one—easy. And you know she can—and will—do it."

Madison brushed angrily at his florid face, swallowed hard. Cupping a hand to his mouth, he shouted: "All of you men—set tight! Don't try nothing on your own. Just hold off for me to give you the word."

The rancher's words echoed faintly in the hush and startled a pair of mourning doves resting in the nearby mesquite into sudden erratic flight.

"That will be the last thing you'll ever do," Rutledge said disapprovingly. "Figured you understood that."

He was studying the men with Madison—one, he saw, was the cowhand who had been with Clint Madison earlier in the day. The others all appeared to be much like him, ordinary, everyday hired help more at home on the range, now accompanying the rancher simply because they had been ordered to. The gunmen, if any were in the party, would be among those Cain had sent off into the brush.

"You're mighty cool setting there knowing you're next to dying," Madison said. "All I got to do is yell out."

"Means we both cash it in if you do—"

Madison wagged his head. "I ain't so sure it'll work out like you say. Could be you won't be in no shape to squeeze the triggers on them irons. Could be you'll take a half a dozen slugs all at once—and there ain't no man alive could stand up against that."

"Maybe, but I'm betting it'll go the way I told you— maybe I ought to even promise you that's how it'll be."

Cain raised his hand slowly, carefully, rubbed at his jaw. He looked worn and haggard and it was clear the death of his son had hit him hard. Also, he had not expected the complications he was encountering at Hetty Judson's. But he was staying with it, knowing that Rutledge held the high cards and hoping, no doubt, that something would occur to tip the scales in his favor.

"Dying don't seem to count much with you," he said.

Rutledge's mouth split into a cynical smile. "Nope, it doesn't. Been standing next to a grave for so long now that it never bothers me any more."

"Means you're a gunslinger. You make your living at killing."

"I reckon it means whatever you want it to," Rutledge drawled.

"Gunslinger," Madison said again. "That was why it was easy for you to shoot down my boy."

"It was his play. I tried talking him out of it. You know

that if your man there told you the truth about what happened."

"He told me—"

"Was your son that made the first move. He's like you—wouldn't listen."

"Ain't none of that makes a damn with me!" Cain Madison shouted. "Nobody is going to murder my boy and get away with it."

Rutledge's shoulders stirred. "Expect that could be wrote down as a fool thing to say. Old as you are you ought to be smarter than that."

"Don't try to bamboozle me, Rutledge! You killed my son! Means I'm going to make you pay—"

"Means you're going to join him if you try," Rutledge cut in softly. "Now, there's been enough talking. Let's get this over with. Make your move."

13

Madison, jaw clamped shut, sweat standing out on his forehead, glanced about nervously at his men. Off to the south a distance, and high overhead in the cloudless, marine-blue sky, a half a dozen vultures soared in lazy, gradually sinking circles as they prepared to converge on some luckless animal, breathing its last for one reason or another.

"No need to fret about your boys horning in," Rutledge said, his voice cool, level. "Mrs. Judson will see that they stay out of it." He hesitated, considered the rancher closely, and added: "I reckon you want this strictly between you and me—right?"

Cain Madison swore, brushed at the sweat. "Hell, you know I ain't got a chance drawing against you! I'd be a fool to try."

"You're the one who came here looking to put a bullet in me—or maybe you were figuring to have your hired hands do it for you when my back was turned."

"I come here aiming to do whatever was necessary!" Madison snapped, without thinking.

A hard smile pulled at Rutledge's mouth. "Then we best finish this here and now. I'm not letting you ride off, Madison, until we've settled it. I don't take to the idea of walking around looking over my shoulder for the rest of my life."

The rancher again swiped at the beads on his face and forehead and let his gaze rest on the muzzles of John Rutledge's pistols, both pointed unwaveringly at him.

"Didn't mean that just the way it sounded," he said, lamely. "What I figured to say was—"

"You came here to kill me for shooting your son," Rutledge broke in. "And you brought along plenty of help to get it done. Only the way it's working out you'll likely be dead, too, before it's done with."

"Well, now, I ain't so sure that—"

"Let's cut the talk, Madison. Let's get this over with. Can shoot it out from the saddle—or we can stand down. I'll leave it up to you."

The tension hanging over the men gathered in the brush-lined lane increased with Rutledge's pressing words, and the stillness that followed seemed to deepen and become more threatening.

"Why don't you just sort of let it ride, Mr. Madison?" It was the cowhand who had been with Clint earlier at the time of the shooting who broke the tight hush. Having seen Rutledge in action, it was evident he knew the rancher wouldn't have a chance, and realizing that Cain had backed himself into a corner, he endeavored to bail him out. "Why don't you let Drace handle it? This here's what you pay him for."

Drace . . . Hetty had said he was Madison's hired gun. Apparently he was away somewhere or the rancher would have brought him along.

"Expect that's the thing to do," Madison said, a grateful note in his tone. "Sure ain't no disgrace for a man to admit he's outclassed at a time like this—leastwise, that's how I see it. Ed'll be back tonight. He's your kind and he'll know how to deal with you."

Rutledge shrugged. "Ought to be you settling this—not somebody that works for you. Was your son that got himself killed."

Cain Madison forced a laugh. "Sure, you'd like for it to be me drawing on you! Know damn well I wouldn't stand a chance."

"You think that when you were on your way here? Seems to me you were all cocked and primed to kill me for gunning your boy. Now you're backing off, aiming to leave it to somebody else."

"Why not? Like Joe there said, it's what I pay Ed Drace for. Why? You getting cold feet now that you know you'll be going up against a man good as you figure you are?"

"I doubt if he is," Rutledge replied blandly, "but I reckon we'll find out."

"Yeh, we sure will," Madison said, and called to the men waiting in the brush to head back to the ranch. "We'll just leave it at that—"

"No, not yet," Rutledge said, motioning with the pistols in his hands for the rancher to remain where he was. "Couple of things I want to tell you."

"Nothing I want to hear from you!" Madison snapped, bold now that the matter of a shoot-out had been shifted from his shoulders.

"You'll listen anyway," the tall rider said. "I'm serving notice on you now—leave Mrs. Judson alone. You're to stop hurrahing her—"

"I ain't about to!" the rancher shot back. "Not ever— not until I get this here piece of land."

Rutledge shook his head and spat in disgust. "You're like a lot of men I've run across. You've already got all the land you can use, but you want more."

"That's right," Madison admitted without hesitation.

"Mind telling me why? She's got only a little place, and it's a long way from your range, I'm told. Why are you so set on getting it?"

"I'll tell you why—when I start out to do something, I don't quit till I got it done."

Rutledge waited silently for the man to finish his explanation. Off in the field beyond the Judson house meadowlarks were whistling. The buzzards, he noted, were no longer in the sky.

"Told myself I was going to own this corner of Texas—the whole corner—and I sure'n hell am! Her place is the only piece of ground left that ain't mine."

Disbelief furrowed John Rutledge's brow. "A corner of Texas—"

"Just what I said—and I ain't letting nothing get in the way of me doing it."

"You're loony, Madison—and you're dead wrong."

"How so?"

"Hetty Judson. She's not selling out to you, and you're not driving her off—not while I'm around."

"Which won't be long—Ed Drace'll see to that. I reckon he's the key to the problem."

Rutledge smiled bleakly. "Don't do any betting on it."

"Would if somebody was wanting to. I've seen Ed working. He's plenty good. Surprises me some that you ain't ever heard of him."

"Surprises me, too, if he's all that good. Can tell him I'm ready any time he wants to call me out. Fact is, hearing you talk about him makes me sort of anxious to meet him."

Madison studied Rutledge thoughtfully. Nearby his

men were shifting restlessly, anxious to be on their way
back to the ranch.

"Yeh, I reckon that's the way you'd look at it," he said.
"You'd be real keen to go up against Ed, shoot it out and
see who's best. It won't matter none to you which one of
you ends up dead."

"Not at all," Rutledge replied. "I'm going to tell you
again—leave the woman alone. Keep your hired help off
her land—"

"Hell with that," Madison cut in. "I want this two-bit
outfit—not because it's worth anything as a ranch but because it's a part of what I aim to have. And I'll get it
somehow."

"Not while I'm working for her—"

"Which ain't going to be for long," the rancher said
and, jerking his head at his men, swung about and headed
back down the trail.

Rutledge remained motionless on his horse, allowing
Madison and his riders to move past him. All were staring
straight ahead, seemingly anxious to avoid his hard
glance. As they went by, he kneed his mount about, and
with pistols still ready in his hand, kept his attention on
them, trusting none of them at all.

Then, when they had rounded a bend in the lane, he
slid his weapons back into their holsters and, pivoting the
little gelding he was riding, struck off through the windbreak to its lower end. Reaching that point, Rutledge
again halted and put his eyes on the trail a mile or so
below.

Shortly Cain Madison and his men appeared, the
rancher in the lead, his riders following two abreast as if
they were a column of cavalrymen. Methodically Rutledge counted them off, finally nodded in satisfaction.

There were nine in all; Madison had attempted no trickery and was not doubling some of his riders back to try and bushwhack him. He was, as he had declared, going to leave it up to Ed Drace to settle matters.

A hard smile once more parted Rutledge's lips and a faint glint came into his pale eyes. Drace—the hired gun— he was looking forward to their meeting.

14

Hetty slowly descended the steps that led down from the roof deck of the house to the porch and, leaning her rifle against the wall, waited for John Rutledge to return. From her elevated position she had been able to see everything that had taken place in the lane, even to those final minutes when he had followed Cain Madison and his men for a time to be certain they were not planning to double back and catch him unawares.

She had been able to hear only a part of what was being said, however. Rutledge had spoken in his usual quiet way and thus she had missed his remarks and had been able to judge their content only by Cain Madison's reaction. It had been different where the rancher was concerned; he customarily spoke at a half shout, thus his words reached her clearly.

Regardless, Rutledge had undoubtedly come out winner at the meeting, despite the odds being all against him. And while Hetty knew that her presence on the roof deck with a rifle handy had lent strength to his position, it was apparent that, by the sheer force of his personality and the threat of his pistols, he had turned Madison away.

Abruptly Rutledge came into view at the end of the yard, riding the black she had provided for him. He had just taken a drink from his bottle of whiskey, which was now almost empty, and as he leaned to the side a bit to restore the container to his saddlebags, he smiled at her. Impulsively she came off the porch, feeling a tightening in her throat as she did, and hurriedly crossed to the corral for which he was heading.

"I'm glad you're all right," she said, unable to think of anything better to say.

He came off the black, nodded. Brushing at his mustache with a finger, he said, "Obliged to you for the help. Showing up there on the roof with your rifle sure changed the odds."

"Not about to let you make a stand against Cain Madison and his bunch alone—specially since it's all because of me."

He began to strip the black, saying nothing until the saddle and bridle were off and hanging on the top bar of the corral and the gelding had wandered on to join the others of his kind in the opposite corner of the enclosure. Then, pulling off his hat, Rutledge mopped at his face with a forearm and returned to the yard where Hetty waited.

"Been doing some thinking about what you said," he began as, side by side, they started for the house.

Hetty detected a lightheartedness, almost a boyish eagerness, in his manner as he spoke. "Does that mean you've decided to go partners with me here on the ranch?" she asked, hopefully.

"Nope, but I figure I ought to hang around for a spell, sort of help out until things level off."

Hetty felt a tinge of disappointment but one blunted by the realization that he would be there with her for a while. And who could say? Maybe he'd change his mind and consent to making it a permanent arrangement. There was always hope.

"I'm glad, John," she said. "It'll mean so much to me—and Willa, too—having you here. What about Madison? Were you able to settle—"

"He was running over with threats," Rutledge replied with a shrug. "Seems he aims to sic some hired gun on me. You mentioned the name—Drace."

Hetty stopped short, concern filling her eyes. "He's a killer—a gunman."

"So?" Rutledge said stiffly.

It had been the wrong thing to say; Hetty saw that immediately as they continued toward the porch and stepped up onto it. Just what he would take offense at was unclear.

"Met a few like him before I came here," he said. "Likely I'll run up against a few more after I've moved on."

He had supreme confidence in his abilities, that was evident, and she guessed he was much more famed and respected in the violent world he frequented than he let on. Hetty cast a sly glance at him as he opened the door for her and stood aside for her to enter. Again she felt that swelling in her throat; *like a schoolgirl with her first crush*, she thought, and silently rebuked herself.

Tall, muscular, deeply tanned from the sun and wind, his pale eyes like bits of blue ice, he suddenly had taken on an aura of danger and excitement.

"I want to tell you again, John, how happy I am that you're going to—to stay," she said, stammering a bit under the steady pressure of his direct gaze. She was repeating herself, she knew, but it didn't matter. "You don't like ranch work and I—"

"Expect I'll survive," he said dryly. "After we've had a

bite to eat you can tell me what you want done and I'll get started at it."

She nodded as he allowed the door to close behind her and turned to go to his own quarters. "I'll call you when dinner's ready."

Hetty noticed that the smell of whiskey on his breath was stronger when he presented himself for the noon meal, but he never showed any effects from drinking and so far had displayed none of the obnoxious traits she ordinarily associated with those who did. They ate in silence. When it was done, he settled back in his chair and, lighting one of his thin, black cigars, gave her direct study.

"I'm waiting to be told what you want done, boss," he said, smiling.

Hetty returned the smile, heaved a deep sigh. "I'm afraid there's lots that needs attention around here, but right now I've got to sell off some stock and raise a bit of money."

"You've got sixty dollars gold to start with—"

Hetty smiled again, recalling the moments when John Rutledge had forced Cain Madison to fork over cash for the damage the riders had done.

"Yes—thanks to you. It'll probably be more than enough to replace the windows and that old shed, but I'll still have to sell off some beef. I've got bills in town that need paying—the feed store, the doctor, Mr. Granville—a couple other places. And I need supplies and a few personal things, not to mention the wages I'll be owing you."

"You can forget that," Rutledge said, blowing a smoke ring at Willa, sitting quietly nearby.

Willa had warmed to John Rutledge considerably since he had first appeared on the ranch, as had he to her. She now seemed utterly fascinated by him, and Hetty guessed it was because he was totally unlike any of the men who had been around the place since Jack was killed. Strong, impressive, and so completely sure of himself, he seemed like a father to her.

"No, I pay what I owe—and I'll owe you for your work," Hetty said.

He shrugged indifferently and she knew that if she did attempt to settle with him for his labor he would somehow manage to avoid accepting it. But that was something she'd face—and handle—when the time came.

"How many steers you figure to sell?"

"Twenty-five or so. There's a cattle buyer who'll pay me ten dollars a head, range delivery. He'll send a couple of men to take them back to where he's building up a herd that he aims to drive to a railhead somewhere. I know I could get more if I went direct to the market, but when I only sell off a few, this is a better deal for me."

Rutledge nodded. "Can understand that. . . . Then what needs doing is to round up twenty-five head—"

"Yes—but it's not as easy as it sounds. My herd has strayed and we're going to have to work the canyons and draws, haze the cattle out of the brush and drive them down to my south range. Need to bring in the calves, too. Won't be many of them, I expect. Between the wolves and big cats—"

"I'm still wondering about that," Rutledge said, making it clear he had strong doubts on the matter. "You want me to start this afternoon?"

Hetty shook her head. "It's a job we'll do together—it's nothing new to me. The fact is I've had to take care of rounding up my stock by myself several times when I couldn't hire any help. Couldn't do much of a job alone, of course, but I managed."

Rutledge smiled, his features reflecting his admiration. "I reckon you'll always do that."

Hetty glanced away self-consciously. What ailed her? She was feeling like a schoolgirl again—she, self-sufficient, utterly capable Hetty Judson—a grown woman, a widow even, and with a child!

"It's been a case of either or else," she said. Then, frowning, she added: "There are a few things—small jobs around the house that I'd like to get done this afternoon."

"We can start tomorrow—"

"Well—no. Tomorrow I need to go into town. The doctor wants to see Willa again—she's been having some trouble with one of her ears. And I have a list of groceries to pick up."

"Fine. We'll make it a day in town and get to work the next day."

"You don't have to make the ride in with us if there's something else you'd rather do—"

She was thinking of Madison, and his hired gunman, Ed Drace—and all the other hard cases who worked for Cain. The rancher would still be angered over the death of his son, as well as smarting from the treatment he had received at the hands of John Rutledge. It could be extremely dangerous for the tall rider to show himself in Jubilee.

"Nope, be a pleasure to ride along. Fact is, there are a couple of things I'm needing myself. Was going to ask if you minded if I rode in tonight but now I'll just hold off till tomorrow."

Hetty said, "Yes, of course, but I was thinking about Madison and that he'll be looking for the chance to get even with you. With all the help he has, the odds are all in his favor. Aren't you a little bit, well—afraid?"

"What's the point of being scared?" Rutledge asked. "Nobody gets out of this life alive—so being scared of dying is a waste of time. . . . There any more of that coffee left?"

Hetty, rising, went to the stove for the pot. Returning, she filled his cup and then paused, looking down at him.

"You're a strange man, John Rutledge. I'm not sure I know how to figure you."

"Be a waste of time, anyway," he said, and raised the cup to his lips.

15

Rutledge was up shortly before dawn the next morning. He noticed the lamplight glowing in the kitchen window as he crossed from the bunkhouse to the barn and realized that Hetty was also up and about. Reaching the hulking building, he immediately went about the business of doing the necessary chores—feeding the cow, throwing down hay from the loft for the horses, spreading grain for the chickens—all tasks that he detested but felt called upon, under the circumstances, to do.

By the time he was finished Hetty Judson was standing in the doorway, a shawl about her shoulders to ward off the crisp chill of the early hours, calling him to breakfast. He responded at once.

Sitting down at the table with Hetty and her small daughter, he waited silently while the customary blessing was asked and then, aware that the woman was studying him with a disturbed frown, began to eat. Finally Hetty broke the hush.

"There something bothering you, John?"

He paused, a forkful of bacon and eggs halfway to his mouth. "Not much at doing yard chores. Fact is I'd rather do most anything else," he said, bluntly.

Hetty's smile was one of relief. "Just leave them to me. I've grown used to them."

"No, I'll look after them," he replied. "How soon will you be ready to pull out?"

"An hour—"

He had resumed his meal. Taking a swallow of coffee, he said, "Good. Soon as I've finished eating I'll hitch up the wagon."

Hetty's features became serious. "Are you sure it's wise —your going into town? Cain Madison all but owns Jubilee, being such a big customer of everybody's."

"I can't see that he makes any difference," Rutledge replied in a tone that indicated the subject was closed.

Within the hour they were in the wagon and moving east along the road to Jubilee. By late morning they were turning into its single, structure-lined street. Their arrival brought about a noticeable change. Men along the board sidewalks, as well as a few women abroad doing their marketing, paused to stare. Several merchants came to the doorways of their establishments and stood rigidly, eying them narrowly, even disapprovingly. It was clear that a report of the trouble Rutledge had encountered with the Madisons and the incident of Clint's death had preceded them.

A hard, half smile pulling down the corners of his mouth, Rutledge drove straight down the center of the roadway, directing the team for the office of the town's physician, Ed Custer, the location of which was pointed out to him by Hetty Judson.

Pulling to a stop in front of the small cottage, Rutledge stepped down, circled the wagon, and assisted Hetty to alight. Willa was already off the seat by then and standing on the walk, waiting.

"You don't back off at all, do you, John?" Hetty said, smiling wanly. "Most men in your position would have

taken a roundabout way, avoided attracting attention.
You choose to come right down the center of the street."

"That bother you?" he asked.

"Not at all, but aren't you just a little bit nervous—or
maybe I ought to say frightened—exposing yourself like
that?"

"Already told you how I felt about being scared of anything. You think I should be?"

Hetty studied him thoughtfully, the blue of her eyes
rich and deep in the strong sunlight. "Not if you don't see
any reason to be," she replied. "Where shall I meet you
when the doctor is finished with Willa?"

"I'll leave the wagon in front of the general store," he
said, and drew out the thick gold watch carried in the
pocket of his shirt—a clean white one closed at the collar
with a black string tie, at the cuffs with silver links, and
held in place at the elbows with red sleeve garters. After
considering the bold Roman numerals on the face of the
timepiece briefly, he returned his attention to the woman.

"You figure a couple of hours will be enough for you
to get your shopping done?"

Hetty said, "It should—"

"Then I'll meet you at the wagon in two hours. After
that we'll go have us a restaurant dinner."

Hetty smiled with pleasure. "That will be fine—a real
treat!"

Rutledge nodded, started to turn away, hesitated. "In
case you need me before then, you'll find me in that saloon down the way—the Sundowner. Looks like it's the
best one in town."

"Yes, I suppose it is," Hetty said with no particular
feeling in her voice and, taking Willa by the hand, en-

tered the yard fronting the physician's combination home
and office, and hurried to the door.

Rutledge shrugged, a faint smile breaking his lips, and
climbed back onto the wagon seat. Taking up the lines,
he cut the horses about and drove the vehicle to the hitch
rack at the side of Granville's General Store a short distance away. There, after securing the team, he dropped
back to the street, halted at the corner of the structure
standing there, and had a better look at Jubilee.

It was a fair town, he saw, with most of the business
concerns and professional offices necessary to accommo-
date the local and surrounding populace present. Again
he made a cursory check of the saloons, decided that his
initial impression was correct—the Sundowner was the
largest and undoubtedly the best.

Delaying no longer, and still conscious of the attention
he was drawing from persons in the stores and the resi-
dences along the way as well as those on the sidewalk, he
stepped out into the street and angled for the saloon, a
half-block distance on the opposite side.

"Hold it!"

The command, terse and to the point, came from off to
his right. Rutledge slowed, halted. Tension building suddenly within him, hands hanging loosely at his sides, he
pivoted. An elderly man, a shotgun hanging from the
crook of his left arm, was coming toward him.

"You talking to me?" Rutledge asked. His manner had
altered, had become cold, and his voice turned dry when
he saw the star pinned to the man's vest pocket.

"Reckon I am," the lawman snapped. "I've got a couple of things to say to you."

Rutledge drew himself up, folded his arms across his
chest, and waited. Several of the town's merchants had

now forsaken their establishments completely, had come out into the street, and joined loitering bystanders already there. All were watching intently, as were several saloon women gathered on the landings and porches of the places where they worked.

"Name's Tom Farwell," the lawman said, coming to a halt.

Somewhere near fifty, Rutledge guessed, he was a tall, lean individual with a narrow, lined face made sharper by the spade beard and down-curving mustache. He had small, gray eyes, wore a slate-gray suit and a high-crowned hat in an obvious effort to make himself appear taller. *An over-the-hill badge-toter who has found himself a little town where he can still be the big noise,* John Rutledge decided, making his assessment.

"I'm marshal here," Farwell continued, studying the tall rider closely as if having thoughts of recognition. "Been told about the ruckus you had with Cain Madison —and how you killed his boy."

"Expect you were told, too, that I tried to side-step throwing down on him. He wouldn't listen."

Farwell frowned. It was clear that bit of information had not been given to him. Evidently, also, he was acquainted with Clint Madison's ways and was not surprised by what had occurred.

"Makes no damn difference to me!" the lawman said gruffly. "Just want you understanding there ain't to be none of that going on here in my town."

"Suits me," Rutledge said.

"You willing to leave your guns at my office while you're here?"

Rutledge smiled coldly, shook his head. "Nope, I'm not,

Marshal. Doubt if you would either if you were standing in my boots."

Farwell made no reply to that. "Just don't want any trouble," he said. "You figuring to stay around here long?"

"For as long as it takes me to do what Mrs. Judson wants done. Appears your good friend Cain Madison's been making it real tough for her to hire on help."

The marshal brushed angrily at his beard. "Don't go shooting off your mouth about something you're plumb ignorant of! Madison don't own me!"

Rutledge smiled humorlessly. "Now, that surprises me some, considering what the lady had to say. I figured he owned the town and about everybody in it."

"Well, you're wrong," Farwell declared flatly. That he was still probing about in his memory for some indication of Rutledge's identity was evident. "Mind telling me your name?"

"Nope. It's Rutledge—John Rutledge."

Farwell digested that, wagged his head. "Name ain't familiar, but your face sure is. I get the feeling that we've met somewheres—or that I've seen you before—maybe a picture. Just can't nail it down."

"I doubt if we've ever met," Rutledge drawled. "I for sure would've remembered you. Expect I look like a lot of other men. . . . You through talking?"

"Yeh, reckon I am. Just want it understood that I won't stand for no shooting in my town."

"What about Madison's bunch? That go for them, too?"

"You're damn right it goes for them! I already told you I ain't working for Madison!" the lawman said, shifting the shotgun from the crook in his arm to a hand. "And anybody says I am's a liar!"

"Was just going from what I've been told," Rutledge said mildly.

"Meaning?"

"For one, Mrs. Judson couldn't get any help from you when her husband got bushwhacked. And, two, you haven't done anything to protect her from Madison and his hired hands who've been killing her stock, hurrahing her place, tearing up her water holes, and such. I expect there've been some other people around here that he took over who could have used the protection of the law, too."

Farwell's lined face was set to stiff lines. "You're forgetting, mister, that I'm only a town marshal. I ain't got no authority outside the town's limits."

"What I'm not forgetting, Marshal, is that she's a widow woman with a small child alone out there and needing help—and you're a man. The hell with your town limits! You should've looked out for her."

"I'm doing my job—the one I'm paid for," Farwell said defensively.

"And you're mighty afraid they'll quit paying you and take away your star if you do anything to rile Cain Madison—"

The lawman's features remained hard-set. "I didn't hear that, Rutledge—if that's what your real name is. And I'm going to say this only once more—I don't want no trouble here. Do your feuding somewheres else—and the sooner you get out of the country—"

"You running me out, Marshal?" Rutledge's voice was soft and smooth, and the small group of men standing nearby stirred nervously as they recognized the threat it conveyed.

"Nope, ain't got no reason to—yet. I'm just saying that everybody'd be better off if you'd keep riding."

"Maybe so," Rutledge said dryly, "but I'm not figuring to until I've done what I can to help the lady."

"You going to work for her?"

"Already have. Madison either ran off or killed off all the others who hired on with her. I don't aim to let him do either one to me."

Farwell gave that thought. "That mean you're set to kill Madison? You've already took care of his boy—"

"Never said I was out to kill him—but I'm not in the habit of backing down. Choice will be up to him, same as it was to his boy. Now, if you want to make something out of that, go ahead," Rutledge stated and, nodding coolly, resumed his walk to the Sundowner Saloon.

16

Rutledge, features taut, disturbed by the possibility that the past, thanks to the zealous efforts of Town Marshal Tom Farwell, might overtake him before he was able to complete—even thwart—his intentions of helping Hetty Judson, reached the porch of the Sundowner.

The platform was narrow and extended the full width of the two-storied structure. Two women, both young but showing wear, lounged against the forward wall, and they, like several men also loitering close by, regarded him with close interest during his approach.

He paid them but little attention as he moved up to the door where two more men, one a large, beefy, balding individual and the other, dark-faced and slender, dropped back a step to allow him to enter. He favored them with a cold, flat-eyed glance and made his way to the bar, taking note while en route of the half-dozen or so card tables with their accompanying chairs, on the far side of the elongated room.

Immediately the beefy man stepped in behind the bar and faced Rutledge. Nodding, he said: "Name's Pete Zell. This here's my place. I'd as soon you'd picked one of the others but since you're here what'll you have?"

"Whiskey—a quart," Rutledge replied.

Zell produced a full bottle, set it on the counter. "Two dollars—"

Rutledge handed a half eagle to him. "Take out for two. I'll take the other with me when I leave."

Zell nodded, slid a silver dollar and a glass across the counter to the tall rider. Drawing the cork of the bottle, Rutledge filled his glass and looked questioningly at the saloon man. Zell shook his head.

"I do my drinking at night—after I get home."

Rutledge's shoulders stirred indifferently. Turning, drink in his hand, he looked out over the room. The dark, slim man was now at one of the tables absently shuffling a deck of cards. Two of the men who had been on the porch were sitting down with him preparing to play. Three others were close by, talking quietly among themselves while the two garishly dressed women had taken up a stand at the end of the bar and were still considering him expectantly.

Rutledge smiled at them in his brief, cool way, said: "Don't waste your time on me," and, pulling away from the counter, crossed to where the gambler and his two opponents were getting set.

"This an open game?" he asked.

The slim man nodded. "You're welcome," he said, and added, "Your name's Rutledge. I overheard. Mine's T. J. Langley—T.J. they call me. And the game's stud poker."

"Suits me," Rutledge said. Taking the vacant chair, he placed the glass of whiskey on the table near his elbow and the bottle on the floor beside his foot.

No introduction was made to or by the other players and Rutledge paid them small notice other than that of a man appraising others over a hand of poker. But the trio who were now lounging against the wall to his left were claiming his covert attention. Two of them, he was certain, had been with Cain Madison the day before when the rancher came with his riders to the Judson ranch. The third man, most likely, was a Circle M employee, too.

Rutledge turned to the man on his right. "You mind changing places with me, friend?"

The man frowned, hesitated, and finally shrugged. "Why not? Maybe it'll bring me some luck," he said, and then after the exchange had been made, added: "There a reason why you're doing this?"

Rutledge downed his glass of whiskey. He was now in a position to keep the three Circle M riders in view at all times, but he shook his head, said, "Nope, just sort of favor this side of the table," and let that serve as his explanation.

The game began, slow and with low stakes. Rutledge drank steadily and smoked continually, neither of which appeared to affect him in any way. The trio of Madison men settled down at a table, ordered drinks and beckoned to the women to join them. Other customers entered the saloon, paused at the bar for a beer or whiskey, and departed, or else continued to hang around to talk with Pete Zell and observe the poker game while casting surreptitious glances at John Rutledge from time to time.

The first hour passed. One of the Circle M riders—the one Rutledge had not seen before—departed as did the player sitting in the game to the dealer's left. He'd had no luck, he declared, and pulled out. Immediately his place was filled by a patron at the bar who was voluble when he first sat down but, upon being stonily ignored by the other players, quickly fell silent and intent on the game.

It grew warm in the hushed saloon. Smoke began to hang in the motionless air and gather about the oil-lamp chandeliers overhead. The smell of whiskey, beer, and sweat, mitigated somewhat by the perfume the women

had liberally applied to their persons, became more pro-
nounced.

Rutledge was an expert. Such became apparent as the
stacks of coins and the number of crumpled bills mounted
before him. Several times the gambler, Langley, looked
up at him thoughtfully as he won a hand, a frown on his
dark, narrow face, but he said nothing. Long ago he had
adopted the philosophy of lose today, win tomorrow
when playing in an honest game.

Finally Rutledge, after glancing at his watch, refilled
his glass once more, downed it, and setting the near-
empty bottle on the table, pushed back his chair and rose
to his feet.

"I'm obliged, gentlemen," he said, nodding to Langley
and the other two players. "Happens I have an appoint-
ment."

"Sure hate hearing that," one of the men said, scrub-
bing at his jaw. "You've got about forty dollars of my
money. Sure would like to get it back—or leastwise, try."

"Another time," Rutledge said, and put his attention on
T. J. Langley. "What's the best restaurant in town?"

"The Dakota—right on down the street," the gambler
replied.

Rutledge signified his thanks for the information and
started to turn and cross to the bar where Zell was waiting with the extra quart of whiskey he'd bought and paid
for. The harsh voice of one of Madison's hired hands
brought him up short.

"Rutledge—you ain't leaving!"

The tall rider, without bothering to come about, shifted
his narrowed eyes to the Circle M man, out of his chair
and standing hard against the wall. His companion was
also on his feet and had assumed a like position a few

strides away while the two women were hastily removing themselves from the immediate area.

The saloon was in a deep hush. Zell, frowning, swiped at the sweat on his broad, florid face with a bar towel and muttered something at low breath. A hard, dry smile cracked Rutledge's mouth as he studied the two Madison men.

"You looking for trouble, boys?"

"You've already got it," the shorter of the pair snapped. "We got you hemmed up in the middle—right where we want you."

"What you're wanting is to die," Rutledge said coldly. "I'll kill you both before you can draw iron. That what you're looking for?"

The rider threw a hurried look to the door as if he were expecting someone to appear. His friend shook his head.

"It ain't going to be all that easy for you—"

"Maybe that's how you see it. I've got a different idea— I'm walking out of here over your dead bodies if I have to. What's this all about? You trying for top hand with Madison by taking on me? If that's it, you'd best forget it. You won't live long enough to have him pat you on the back."

"That's mighty big talk—"

"I mean every word of it. I'll say it again, forget it."

"The hell with that!"

Rutledge's stance altered. His head came forward slightly and his eyes closed down even more as he pivoted slowly. "Don't make the same mistake Clint Madison did," he warned softly.

"They ain't going to!" Pete Zell said from the end of the bar. "Not here in my saloon, anyway!"

The bar owner came out from behind his counter. He

was holding a double-barreled shotgun in his hands and
there was little doubt in his manner that he would use the
weapon if it became necessary.

"Daily," he said, glaring at the shorter of the two men,
"you and Ike get the hell out of here! And don't be coming back unless you come peaceable."

Daily hung motionless and stiff-faced for a long breath
and then, throwing a look at his friend, allowed his squat
shape to relax. He nodded sullenly at Zell.

"You ain't got no call butting in on this, Pete! This
here's Circle M business, and I aim to tell Mr. Madison
that you—"

"You can tell him any damn thing you please!" the saloon man cut in angrily, "but while you're doing it don't
you forget to tell him that I probably saved your fool
neck—Ike's, too. You'd both be dead right now if I hadn't
horned in."

"Maybe," Daily said, starting to move toward the door.
"I'm warning you, Pete—Mr. Madison ain't going to like
this!"

Zell shrugged his thick shoulders. "I can't help that—
I'm just looking out for my business."

Daily and Ike slouched by, casting hard glances at
Rutledge as they did. They reached the doorway, paused
to look back, and then stepped out onto the porch and beyond sight. Immediately the tension and hush within the
saloon broke and Rutledge, head coming up, shoulders
squaring, continued to the bar. Claiming his bottle of
whiskey, he smiled at Zell.

"Obliged to you—but it wasn't necessary."

The barman returned the shotgun to its place under the
counter and shook his head. "Wasn't doing it for
you—was for them two damn fools. I didn't want to see

them get their selves killed. Now, there's a back door if you're of a mind to use it. They could be hanging around out front—waiting."

Rutledge gave that thought. He was aware that the saloon had again become quiet, as the men at the bar, the women, and the gamblers had paused to note his reaction. After a bit he shrugged.

"Obliged again," he said, tucking the bottle of liquor under an arm, "but I reckon not. There's a lady expecting me at the general store. Best I go out the front way."

Zell's heavy shoulders lifted and fell. Picking up a towel, he began to mop at the surface of his counter. "Up to you. Luck," he murmured.

Rutledge bobbed crisply and walked on toward the door. He was not taking the saloonkeeper's veiled warning lightly. The probability that Daily and Ike—and possibly other Circle M men scouted up by the rider who had left the place earlier—could be waiting for him was very real.

But it was not in John Rutledge to dodge the likelihood by ducking out the back door. If he was to have it out with them, it might as well be then and there—and he certainly didn't want them laying an ambush along the trail somewhere when he headed back with Hetty Judson and her daughter in the wagon with him.

He reached the open doorway and paused. A surge of caution swept through him, mingling with a thread of heady excitement. They were out there—just as Pete Zell had suggested they might be. But there were four of them now: Daily, Ike, the rider who had taken his leave—and a fourth man.

17

Rutledge moved through the doorway, halted again. He
threw a quick glance toward Granville's store. Hetty and
her small daughter were standing beside the wagon waiting for him. The street, otherwise, had cleared, as persons
seeing the four men drawn up in its center and sensing
imminent violence had hurried to take cover.

"They went and got Ed Drace—"

The voice came from behind Rutledge. He realized
that Pete Zell and likely all the patrons of his saloon had
collected in its entrance where they would have a good
view of what was about to take place.

Drace . . . Cain Madison's hired killer. The rancher
had said he'd bring him in, and he had. Evidently that
morning the gunman had been somewhere in Jubilee,
probably at one of the other saloons, and the Circle M
rider who had left the Sundowner earlier had gone in
search of him. That he had found Drace was also apparent, and he had undoubtedly told him that the man
Madison wanted him to kill was right there in town, in
the Sundowner where Ike and Daily were keeping him
occupied.

A bleakness had settled over John Rutledge's features
and a brightness, almost an eager anticipation, filled his
eyes. His wide shoulders pitched forward slightly, tightening the seams of his white shirt and suddenly there was

about him the coiled, deadly look of a man about to strike, to kill quickly, mercilessly. Without taking his narrowed gaze off the men in the street, he thrust the bottle of whiskey he'd purchased at the group in the doorway behind him.

"Hold this," he said in a lead-cold, authoritative tone. Giving no thought to the person accepting it, he dismissed it from his mind and walked farther out onto the porch in a deliberate, gliding sort of step. Reaching the edge of the landing he came to a stop.

"Well?" he called quietly.

The men in the street stirred. The stranger, the one who could only be Drace—a squat, thick man wearing among other items a pair of new boots, eased forward a step.

"I'm Ed Drace," he drawled. "That mean something to you?"

Rutledge, shoulders still forward, hands now hanging at his sides, shook his head. "Nothing."

"Well, it sure ought—"

Tension lay over the deserted street like a warm, suffocating cloud. The hush was equally oppressive. Rutledge continued to stare at the gunman, drilling the man relentlessly with his pale, sharp eyes. Daily, standing at Drace's left, shifted nervously, took a half step to the side. The other Madison riders had already spread out, thus making it clear they intended to back the gunman's play.

Rutledge's mouth twisted into a hard grin. He knew now how it was to be. Raising his eyes but a very little he placed them on Hetty. She had not moved, was still standing near the wagon.

"Get inside—stay there!" he said, raising his voice.

He saw the woman hasten to comply and immediately returned his full concentration to the Circle M men in the street. The quiet, broken by his shout to Hetty Judson, was again blanketing the street.

"You know what you're doing?" he said then to Drace.

The gunman nodded. "Can bet your bottom dollar I do."

"You know why?" Rutledge persisted, his voice low, almost regretful.

"Got a couple of reasons," Drace replied. "I reckon it's mostly on account of Clint Madison. He was a friend of mine."

"That's one reason. What's the other?"

Drace frowned, brushed impatiently at his whisker-stubbled jaw. The heat from the driving sun, aided and abetted by the tension, was making itself felt in the narrow, dusty canyon between the two walls of false-fronted buildings.

"Expect that's my business—"

"Yes, I suppose it is," Rutledge said, coming slowly off the porch and down to street level. "But whatever it is, it's going to cost you your life. Smart thing for you to do is turn around and walk off—right now."

Drace's eyes flared with surprise and anger. He glanced at Daily and then at Ike and the third rider, and forced a laugh.

"Yeh, that's just what I'll do—back down to the likes of you! I ain't paid to back down—and I sure'n hell don't need to this time."

"Up to you," Rutledge said and then, as if suddenly remembering, raised his eyes for a look at the marshal's office.

The door was closed, and there was no sign of Tom Farwell. Either the lawman had earlier ridden out of town for some reason, or else, at the first hint of trouble, had found other matters to occupy his attention.

"We settling this or you aiming to talk me to death?" Drace asked after a time.

Rutledge smiled coldly. "I'm waiting on you. . . . What about your friends there? They cutting themselves in on it?"

Drace glanced at the three men near him, shook his head. "Not far as I'm concerned—I sure'n hell don't need no help. What they do is purely up to them."

"It sure is!" Daily declared in a loud voice. "If'n Ed here don't blow your damned head off, me and the boys aim to. Maybe you don't know it, mister big noise, but you've plain come to the end of your rope."

Rutledge's expression did not change. "I should've let you have your try back there inside the saloon a bit ago," he said. "Wouldn't have you snapping at my heels now."

"They won't get in the way," Hetty Judson announced from the sidewalk. "I'll see to that."

Rutledge, eyes still locked on Drace, allowed himself a quick glance at the woman. Rifle leveled and hammer cocked, she was off to his left a few strides. Drace and the other Madison riders had been unaware of her approach, also, and now all but the gunman had turned and were staring at her.

"Drop your guns," she ordered, "then back away. This is between my foreman and Drace. I won't have you butting in."

The rider named Ike spat into the dust. "And what if we've got other notions, lady. What'll you do?"

"This," Hetty replied and triggered a bullet into the ground at the Circle M rider's feet.

Ike yelled and jumped back as the echoes bounced along the street. Dogs began to bark excitedly and somewhere a man yelled as if startled by the sound.

"You need any more proof?" Hetty asked quietly.

For answer Ike and the two other men carefully drew their weapons, allowing them to fall into the loose dust.

"Now back off—"

Mumbling curses all three riders slowly retreated. Drace, now alone, did not stir, his attention never wavering from the half-crouched, threatening figure of John Rutledge.

A surge of emotion, something closely akin to admiration, or perhaps it was of pride, had swept through John Rutledge when he heard Hetty Judson's words and caught a glimpse of her standing nearby ready to back his play. But the diversion of thought was only fleeting, occupied but a fragment of time. Experience had long ago taught him that a break in concentration on the matter at hand could be fatal if prolonged over a brief instant.

"I reckon that ought to satisfy you," Drace said. "Ain't no need for you to fret no more about the odds being against you."

"It wasn't bothering me all that much," Rutledge countered. "Just needed to know where I stood. Would be a shame to kill three innocent men just because they happened to be along with you."

Drace's eyes showed irritation for the first time. His mouth tightened and a frown pulled at his forehead, causing the beads of sweat collected there to stand out more prominently.

"You're mighty damn sure of yourself!" he said.

"That's what keeps me alive," Rutledge answered.

"Well, it ain't going to work this time!" Drace shouted and made a sudden stab for his pistol.

The gunman was fast. There was no doubt of that but

he was no match for John Rutledge. The tall man hardly moved, it seemed to those who were watching. There was only a brief blur of white shirt sleeves, and next the two bone-handled pistols were firing, their dual explosions blending into one thunderous crash.

Drace, his weapon out of the holster but not up and leveled, rocked back on his heels as bullets smashed into his body. He hung there, posed, half bent over as the dogs, stirred into excitement again by the sound of gunshots, began to bark anew. And then abruptly, he twisted to one side and fell heavily into the dust.

Rutledge, motionless, smoke trickling from the muzzles of his pistols and curling about him, raised his narrowed eyes slowly and let them stop on Daily and the two Circle M riders standing with him. They were frozen, mouths agape from shock and astonishment.

"Pick him up," Rutledge ordered in a chilled voice. "Don't leave him laying there in the dirt."

Daily bobbed hastily and, beckoning to Ike and the other rider, hurriedly moved to the gunman's prone body.

"Take him straight to Madison. Tell him I said to let it end here. It's already cost him too much."

Again Daily nodded. He stooped, started to pick up his pistol, hesitated, and glanced uncertainly at Rutledge.

The tall man nodded. "All right—long as you holster it and leave it there. Try to use it and I'll kill you, too."

The Circle M rider shook his head to signify he had no such intentions and Rutledge turned away. Putting away his own weapons, he shifted his attention to Hetty Judson, waiting, rifle in hand, close by. Taking the long gun from her, he smiled.

"Let's go eat," he said. "Expect you're a mite hungry by now."

18

Walking at the side of John Rutledge as he strode purposefully toward the wagon pulled up at Granville's, Hetty stole a quick look around. People were coming out into the street now, some gathering in small groups to talk about the shooting, others walking over to where two of the three Madison riders were hunkered about the body of Ed Drace; the third Circle M man had apparently been sent to bring up the horses.

In the still tense hush, Rutledge was seeing none of it. He was looking straight ahead, she noted, when she slid a glance at him. He seemed perfectly at ease, a half smile on his lips, his pale eyes soft and partly closed.

Hetty shuddered in spite of herself. She had pegged John Rutledge for a man expert with the pistols he wore—a gunman in fact—after she'd seen him in action. But it hadn't really sunk into her mind what that really meant when it applied to him—a cold, nerveless killer unaffected in the slightest degree by killing—until she had stood there close to him in the street and, fascinated, watched him match ability with another of his kind and coolly come out the victor.

It was a bit frightening. He was like a machine, incapable of error or failure and utterly invincible. Yet he was a gentle man, considerate and courteous, and was probably better educated and knew a more genteel upbringing than

anyone else she had ever met. How did one figure a man
such as he? Did a person just go ahead, accept the—

Hetty's thoughts halted and Rutledge's step slowed as
the sound of running feet, coming from behind, reached
them. She saw the cords in his neck tighten, his eyes shut
down a trifle more and his arms settle at his sides.
Abruptly he pivoted, facing the way they had come. A
man approached them at a run.

"This here's yours," the man, little more than a boy,
called. He was holding a bottle of whiskey in one hand,
now extended toward Rutledge. "You told me to take this
—back there at the Sundowner—to hold it for you."

Hetty saw Rutledge's hard, chiseled visage break and a
faint smile part his lips. Taking the bottle, he nodded.

"Did, for a fact. Had about forgot it. Obliged."

"You're sure welcome, Mr. Rutledge," the man said
and, wheeling, hurried off.

"I'm asking another favor," the tall rider called after
him. "If the marshal wants to see me, I'll be with my two
ladies in the restaurant—the Dakota."

"Yes, sir, I'll tell him. But he won't be. He rode off right
after I seen him talking to you. I wouldn't be knowing
where he went."

Hetty smiled secretly. *With my two ladies,* Rutledge
had said. It was like him to put it that way. How could a
man so polite, so thoughtful, be so cold-blooded, have
such low regard for life, not only that of others but of his
own?

They had reached the wagon and Willa, bursting from
the doorway of the store, was running across the landing
to meet them. Rutledge, winking at her, laid the rifle on
the floor in its customary place under the seat and stowed
the bottle of whiskey into one of the boxes of groceries

that Granville had loaded. Then, turning, he caught the little girl under the arms and swung her up onto the wagon. He was in high, good spirits, Hetty saw, and she realized at that moment the reason for such was not that he'd killed a man but that he was the winner of a deadly contest.

"I'm betting you're starved," she heard him say as the child laughed. "Well, missy, we're going to fix that right now!"

Hetty watched him come about on a heel and put his attention on her. His eyes were open now, and while there was still an iciness in their pale depths, they were bright.

"I reckon it wouldn't be proper to lift you up to the seat like that—not with all these folks gawking at us—so I'll just offer my hand."

Hetty smiled, accepted, and he assisted her onto the wagon. His fingers had been firm and steady, and, other than the glint in his eyes, he showed no signs of excitement or reaction to what he'd just been through.

When she was seated, he stepped aboard and, cutting the vehicle around, drove down the street to the Dakota restaurant and pulled up to the hitch rack erected at its north side. The men from the Circle M had gotten the body of Ed Drace onto a horse, she saw, and were moving slowly off along the south road, taking it, as Rutledge had directed, to Cain Madison.

As she allowed him to lower her from the wagon and had turned to help Willa, Hetty wondered if Madison would heed the words John Rutledge had told the men to convey—to let the trouble end there with the death of Ed Drace.

It was possible, she told herself, hopefully. Cain had

lost a son, had received short shrift at the hands of Rutledge, and now experienced the death of his hired killer,
a man he probably had felt certain would remove the tall
gunman from his path.

It would be wonderful if Madison would listen and
agree. There had been enough killing—for her sake—and
she wanted no more. Not that she was forgiving Cain
Madison for what he had done to her—that would never
come to pass—but there was being too much blood
spilled, and maybe, if things would level off, John Rutledge might—

"You've got a mighty hungry daughter and hired hand
here waiting, ma'am—"

Hetty came back to the moment with a start at the
sound of his voice. She laughed, marveling again at his
ease and great good humor after the incident in the
street. Moving out ahead of him, she crossed the porch of
the restaurant and entered.

The Dakota had few customers. There were two men at
the counter and a man and a woman at one of the tables.
All turned, gave them a quick, shuttered glance, and
looked away. Haughtily ignoring them, Hetty set a course
for a back corner of the room where they would not be on
display, and all sat down.

A waitress appeared shortly, took their orders, and retreated into the kitchen. While the food was being prepared she relieved the delay by bringing coffee for the
adults and a glass of milk for Willa who wrinkled her
nose in a show of distaste when it was placed before her.

"I'll make you a deal," Rutledge said, smiling. "You
drink that and eat everything on your plate and I'll treat
you to a sarsaparilla."

The frown on Willa's face vanished and immediately

she reached for the milk and began to sip it. Rutledge grinned.

"Never took much stock in bribes—but maybe it's a good idea sometimes."

Minutes passed and the meal came. Hetty, forsaking her deep thoughts, began to eat, enjoying the food as were Rutledge and Willa. As to her own opinion, it was fair; the meat was too well cooked, the gravy lumpy, and the fried potatoes only so-so. But it was a dinner prepared by someone other than herself away from her own kitchen, and that in itself was a treat.

Finished with their plates, and after they had dawdled over second cups of coffee and Willa had had her sarsaparilla, they returned to the wagon. Settling themselves on the seat, and again driving down the center of the street where curious faces peered out at them from windows and doors, they began the long journey back to the ranch.

If Rutledge had any fears of ambush along the road he did not reveal them. To the contrary, he laughed and joked with Willa and Hetty all the way, telling little stories, quoting from his favorite books, and seemingly thoroughly enjoying himself.

Hetty fell to wondering if such was the sort of reaction that always claimed him after a scene of violence—one of jubilation. If true it gave rise to a terrible question: did John Rutledge take pleasure in killing? Did it make him happy to take the life of another human being?

The thought lodged in Hetty's mind like a shadow trapped in the late afternoon's glow, and immediately began to haunt her. And even after they had reached her ranch without interruption, and he had unloaded the wagon, stabled the horses, and gone on to his quarters in the bunkhouse, it continued to trouble her.

But later when supper was over and Willa had gone to her bed and Rutledge was taking his ease on the porch, Hetty discovered that the horrifying possibility had faded from her mind, that it actually didn't matter. She knew him as a man otherwise and, womanlike, now deliberately blinded herself to any faults and shortcomings and accepted him as he was to her.

"About time I was getting some work done around here," he said, relighting his cigar as she sat down on the opposite end of the step. "Man's got to earn his keep."

"You have—already," she murmured.

He looked up from the tip of his stogie and considered her with faint amusement. "Some things a man doesn't count as work. I want to talk about what you want done. There's a chance I might have to ride out before too long, and I don't want to leave you in a hole."

19

Hetty Judson had paused and become still and tense. "Leave?" she said, frowning. "I knew you intended to go, but somehow I—I never figured it would happen."

She paused and watched him blow smoke into the motionless air.

"Why must you?" she continued. "I know it's not because of Madison."

"No, not him," Rutledge replied.

"Is it the law? Are the Rangers looking for you?"

He shrugged. "I guess you could say that—"

"And you're afraid Marshal Farwell recognized you and will notify them that you're here."

"About what it adds up to," he admitted.

He was reluctant to talk of it, that was certain, but Hetty's curiosity had been aroused—not so much for the usual reasons but because of the deep interest in him that she had developed.

"Has it always been like this for you—this being on the run all the time?"

"Not exactly," he said. "There's been a few times when the law and I were on speaking terms—but I'm mighty careful to not fall into the habit."

Hetty stirred, smoothed the folds of her dress where it lay across her knees. "Were you ever married, John?"

It took considerable time for him to reply. He sat motionless staring off into the darkness, the cigar held between a thumb and forefinger of one hand, smoke drifting lazily from its glowing tip. Off in the nearby windbreak a bird chirped sleepily.

"Yes—once. Her name was Lacey."

"Oh? What happened—or don't you want to talk about it—"

Rutledge's shoulders relented. He took several puffs of his cigar and continued to probe the night with unseeing eyes.

"She was a Louisiana girl—tall like you, had dark hair and blue eyes—same as you. It was a family thing, her folks and mine, and we grew up figuring to marry some day. It wasn't like the usual arrangement you hear of—we would have gone ahead and got married even if our folks had been against it.

"After we did, we moved to the ranch over in east Texas that my folks were giving us as a wedding present. But the war came along about that time and turned everything, including our big plans, upside down. When it was over I got back there fast as I could but it was too late. A bunch of renegades—deserters had come along one day looking for money and anything else they might steal and sell somewhere. There was some shooting. I had a couple of old cowhands who'd worked for my father working for me—they were too stove up to go to war. They tried to drive the deserters off and in the shoot-out Lacey was killed along with both of them.

"That's what I came home to—the only woman in the world I ever gave a rap for—dead. I forgot all about our plans and started out to hunt down the renegades. There were four of them; I caught up with them in Kansas."

"Did you kill them?" Hetty asked when he did not finish.

"All four," he replied. "That put me on the wrong side of the law even though they were outlaws, and started lawmen to looking for me. I rode back into Texas and just started loafing around, working when I felt like it, doing a lot of gambling and such. Without Lacey I figured life wasn't worth a plugged copper so I kept on drifting, leaving Texas again and heading off into any direction that took my fancy."

Hetty sighed quietly, shook her head. "I'm sorry about Lacey. I thought there must be something like that back in your past, something sad that turned you, made you, well, like you are. And there's no accounting for what happened to you and Lacey.

"It always seems so unfair, so unjust—like me losing my husband, Jack. That hit me terribly hard. I was at loose ends, too, after that happened, and I guess if it hadn't been for Willa I might have done something desperate.

"But then one day the preacher of the Methodist church in town who had come out and said words over Jack's grave, dropped by to talk. I guess I sort of let go. He let me get it out of my system—about how unfair it all was—and then started talking to me about having to carry on, keep on living no matter what happens to us."

"Talk comes easy to somebody who's not up against the problem—"

Hetty nodded. "I know, and about the only comfort I could take from what he said was that there was no explaining some things—like why Jack had to be murdered in the prime of his life—and that we could never really know the answer. God, I remember him saying, undoubtedly had a motive because He moved in mysterious ways to—"

"God never did anything for me except tear out my heart," Rutledge cut in bitterly, tossing the cold cigar butt off into the yard. "What do you want me to start doing first tomorrow?"

It was full dark by then but the night was warm and the scent of lilacs filled the air.

"I expect we'd better start rounding up strays and driving them down to the lower range where the rest of the stock is. There are always a lot of steers hiding out up there in those brushy draws."

Popping strays out of the brush was one of John Rutledge's least favorite tasks but he had let himself in for whatever was needed and thus he did not comment on the fact.

"I'll get at it right off in the morning," he said. "Just tell me how to get there."

"No need—I'll be riding with you."

Rutledge twisted about, shook his head. "Probably be better if you stayed here with the little girl—"

"You think Madison will try something?"

"No way of knowing, I reckon, what any man'll do when things all go wrong for him. Some just sort of accept it, others go a bit loony, start looking for ways to hit back."

"Well, it doesn't matter," the woman said. "Willa is here alone most of the time while I'm off working. She's been told what to do if trouble comes."

"But a five-year-old girl—"

"Six—and don't fret over her. She knows she's to stay inside the house when I'm not around, and if she sees someone coming she's to use the rifle—warn them off. I taught her how to shoot—and she's plenty good for her size."

Rutledge smiled. "Can agree to that."

"The shots serve two purposes. They keep back anyone approaching the house, and they warn me that something's wrong. My ranch isn't so large that I can't hear the gunshots and get here fast."

"It's a good plan," Rutledge said, "but what happens if some jasper gets by her shots and makes it to the house before you can get here?"

"Willa knows to hide in a closet or under a bed— somewhere. And as I've said, I'll get here quick."

Rutledge shrugged, accepting her words. Down near the barn an owl hooted in its lonely, forlorn way. He listened idly, then said, "I guess you know what you're talking about but it just doesn't seem right leaving a youngster like her here alone—"

"You're forgetting that it's been that way ever since I lost Jack. It had to be—I didn't have a choice. I tried taking her with me at the start but it didn't work out—she's small and she tires easily. I want to round up what calves are running loose tomorrow, too, and drift them down to where they can be branded. It won't be much of a job. Like I've told you, there's never many left by this time— thanks to the wolves and cougars—but every one counts."

"I aim to look into that," Rutledge said. "Seems to me you ought to be having a good calf crop with all this feed and water, and you haven't had a hard winter in this part of the country for years."

"That's true, but the tally never comes up to expectations."

Rutledge stirred, drew himself erect, stretched, and stood for a time silhouetted against the darkness beyond.

Hetty studied him thoughtfully and finally got to her feet, also.

"John, I forgot to thank you for the dinner. It was a treat."

"My pleasure," he said in his quiet, faintly accented voice. "It in no way comes up to your kind of cooking but I figured the change would suit you."

"It did—every minute of it," Hetty said, obviously taking pains to not mention the encounter with Ed Drace. "Are you going to read for a while before you turn in?"

Rutledge nodded. "Habit of mine."

She moved forward a step that she might look into his face. "Will you read to me from one of your books if I drop by?"

"That would be my pleasure, too. Any special one?"

"I—I think I'd like to hear something from the *Rubaiyat*—"

He nodded. "Khayyam sounds good to me, too."

"Fine. I'll be there as soon as I look in on Willa."

20

"I own everything from the gate in front of my place to those hills to the west and that line of red bluffs in the north," Hetty Judson said, pointing. It was still early morning when they halted in the sharp, half light on a knoll a mile or so from the house.

"There's better than forty thousand acres of deeded land, and it's almost all good grass."

Rutledge nodded appreciatively. "How far south do you go?"

"You can't see it from here but there's a creek that cuts across a fair-sized valley down there. It's my south line." The woman paused, sweeping the country before them with her eyes. "I know my place isn't big compared to a lot of ranches, but what I've got is good and it's all I want. And for certain it's all I can handle alone."

"A fine place, all right," Rutledge commented. "Madison said he wanted it because he aims to own this corner of Texas. I've got a hunch there's more to it than that. Looking things over, my guess is that he wants it for winter range."

Hetty smiled tightly. "He'll never get it as long as I'm able to stand in his way."

"And knowing his kind, he'll never quit trying," Rutledge said. Then, "We go clean up to the bluffs and start working back this way, that it?"

"No need to go that far. The stock usually doesn't do that much drifting. Most of it'll be found in those draws you can see below that ridge to the west. There's a spring at the head of the main canyon that keeps a little creek flowing catty-corner across the flats, and since there's always plenty of grass, the cows sort of stick around that part of the range."

Rutledge nodded, said, "I reckon the best way to get them out of there is to start hazing." Roweling his new horse—the black gelding he'd gotten from Cain Madison as payment for his sorrel, he struck off through the low hills.

The thought was running through his mind that the sooner the disagreeable job was done, the sooner he'd be able to return to and start enjoying the preferable things in life.

Hetty caught up with him by the time he had reached the narrow flat that lay below the brush-filled draws and arroyos. Signaling to her that he would take the upper end, he rode on.

Shortly he came to the creek she had mentioned and, halting there to let the black slake its thirst, he gave the country before him a quick study.

It was easy to see why Hetty's cattle would seek out the upper range. It was smooth and grass-covered, with chinaberry, pecan, and other trees scattered about, providing shade from the summer sun and a bit of shelter against the winds of winter. A stream of clean water coursed down one side. There could be no better place for stock to thrive.

And all should be in prime condition, Rutledge thought, as he put the black into motion once again.

Hetty Judson would have no trouble getting top prices for her beef regardless of where she marketed it.

He swung wide, gained the upper end of the draws, noting from time to time the upthrust head of a steer visible in the ragged brush and marking his passage with baleful eyes. They would all be half wild and driving them out of their hiding places would be no easy chore.

Such proved to be only too true, and two hours later, after he'd worked the draws within a space of a mile, Rutledge found himself and the black with only a small number of steers to show for their efforts.

But he kept at it, and by the time he caught up with Hetty, working the lower draws, he'd more than doubled the number. Those added to the dozen or so that the woman had hazed out of the brush made for fairly good results, since they, together, had covered only about a third of the draws involved.

"Sure is a funny thing though," he said after Hetty had commented on their middling success, "I haven't spotted a calf yet—not one."

They had pulled up under one of the spreading trees to rest their horses, as well as themselves, for a few minutes. The cattle they had collected were bunched and were now moving slowly across open ground for the south range.

"That's what I've been telling you," Hetty said. "I always come up short."

"Have you ever seen a wolf or a big cat up here?"

She shook her head. "No—I've heard wolves howling but I've never seen one. The same goes for cougars."

"I kept looking for sign—mostly along the creek. Wasn't any—and there should be tracks or the leavings of a kill."

Hetty frowned and brushed at the sweat on her cheeks.

"There would be at that—and I've never come across either."

Rutledge also swiped at the beads on his face. "With this kind of range there ought to be plenty of calves. Even if the wolves and cats got a few, you still ought to end up with a fair tally."

Hetty's shoulders lifted, fell resignedly. She sighed. "Makes sense all right, but it never works out that way."

The tall rider gazed off across the flat, his lean face knotted thoughtfully. After a bit he turned and moved toward his horse.

"Keep your eyes peeled from here on for sign," he said. "Should turn up some—along with a few calves. If we don't—"

Hetty, crossing to her mount, took up the reins, thrust a foot into a stirrup, and prepared to go onto the saddle. She paused, waiting for him to finish.

"If we don't—what?" she prompted when he did not complete his comment.

"Then you've got somebody living off your calf crop," he said, and swung onto the black.

Hetty shrugged, finished mounting. "I know most ranchers don't bother much with calves, but with a small operation like I've got, they really count. I hope we—"

She broke off abruptly as Rutledge, sitting rigidly upright on the black gelding, suddenly raised a hand for silence. Hetty caught the sound, too, immediately—a distant, almost inaudible bawling.

"Not steers," she said after a bit, looking quickly at Rutledge. "Too high pitched. You think it could be calves?"

"Only one way to find out for sure," he answered and,

raking the black with his spurs, rushed off across the grassy plateau at a fast lope.

Hetty quickly caught up and ranged in alongside. "What—" she began.

Rutledge shook his head and shortly reined his horse down to a fast walk while keeping the animal on the grass to deaden the sound of hoofs. The bawling was much louder now and appeared to be coming from a wide arroyo off to their right.

"Best we go quiet until we can see what's going on," he said. "Just could be we've come across what you're looking for—the reason why you never have many calves."

Hetty Judson made no reply, but kept in close to him as they drew near the broad, sandy-floored wash. Brush lined the banks, forming near-solid walls. Minutes later, with the bawling filling the dusty air, they saw color and motion that quickly, upon closer observation, melded into a small herd of two dozen or so calves being driven by two riders.

Again Rutledge made a sign for quiet, and cutting away, he circled wide, swung in, and came to a stop in the dense growth at the edge of the arroyo some hundred yards or so below the oncoming herd. Dismounting, he helped Hetty down from her saddle, and then together they moved in to where they had a clear view of the wash.

The calves, bunched together for mutual consolation, appeared almost immediately. They were in the center of the broad arroyo, with the men trailing close behind.

"I reckon we've found out why you've never had much of a calf crop," Rutledge said, pushing his hat to the back of his head. It had grown steadily warmer as the morning wore on toward noon, and beads of sweat, clouded with dust, were again on his face. "You know either one of those jaspers?"

Hetty, her lips compressed into an angry, straight line, nodded. "One with the brown hat is named Ed Howe. He's a cowhand who works for Madison. Other one they call Benjie. He's just a loafer—lays around the saloons in town. He's sort of simple-minded."

"Seems they've hired themselves out in the cattle business," Rutledge said. "It's sure going to be interesting to know who they sell to." He turned, looking at the woman. "Best you stay right here; let me handle this. Rustlers don't like getting caught in the act and usually try to shoot their way out."

"I'll stay clear," Hetty said, reluctantly, making no stronger promise than that.

Rutledge let it drop and, waiting until the calves had passed and the two riders, slouched in their saddles, a pipe in the mouth of one, the butt of a cigar clamped between the teeth of the other, were abreast, then stepped suddenly out of the brush into the wash.

"Your cattle drive ends here, boys," he announced.

Both men jerked upright and struggled to control their startled, shying horses.

"I'm advising you both to forget those guns you're wearing," he continued, as the riders got their mounts quieted down. "You even look like you want to draw them and I'll kill you."

"I—I ain't about to!" Benjie shouted through the drifting dust. His eyes were spread wide by fear.

Rutledge nodded coldly. "You're being smart. Just unbuckle your belt, let it drop."

Benjie complied hastily. Howe remained motionless, however, seemingly debating the situation and deciding his best course of action. Rutledge considered him narrowly.

"I'm talking to you, too, mister. Don't make a mistake. You've been caught cold-turkey rustling, and shooting you down will be considered good politics. Best you show some good sense—like your partner—and throw down your gun."

Howe gave that thought while the calves, noisily bawling every step, continued on down the arroyo.

"The hell with that!" he yelled suddenly, reaching for his pistol. "I'd sure rather get shot than hung!"

21

Hetty flinched at the sudden blast of John Rutledge's pistol. Standing in the brush at the edge of the arroyo, she had pulled her rifle from the saddle boot and had it ready in her hands in the event Rutledge needed help. The shot had, nevertheless, taken her unexpectedly and, now taut, she stepped down into the wash.

A tremor ran through her—one of vast relief. Ed Howe was sliding from his horse and falling to the ground. The front of his checked shirt was rapidly staining with blood. No doubt he was dead instantly.

There was no need to fear for Rutledge, she saw. He was slack in his saddle, smoking pistol rigid in his hand. Eyes partly closed, skin pulled tightly over the bones of his face and shining dully in the sunlight, there was the ghost of a smile on his lips. Again that unwelcome thought slipped into her mind; John Rutledge killed easily, almost joyfully and it left him totally devoid of remorse—yet he was a kind and gentle man willing to go to any length, without thought of pay, to help her. How could such a contrast exist in one man?

"You going to talk, Benjie?" she heard him say. "I'd as soon haul two dead rustlers to town as one."

Benjie hastily dropped from the back of his horse and, bobbing frantically, said, "I ain't going to give you no trouble, Sheriff!"

Rutledge laughed, rodded the spent cartridge from the cylinder of his pistol, reloaded it, and slid the weapon back into the holster. A short distance down the wash the calves had halted and were looking around uncertainly.

"I'm not the sheriff—I'm the devil's avenging angel," Rutledge said. "And I'm out after the likes of you and your friend there."

"Was all his doing," Benjie declared, staring at Howe's sprawled body.

Hetty walked in closer, the rifle cradled in her arms, watching the man wheel anxiously to her. His whisker-darkened face was contorted and his eyes rolled with fear.

"You know me, Mrs. Judson! I ain't a bad one—you know that! I'm just poor old Benjie that ain't never done—"

"You partnered Howe there in the rustling," Rutledge cut in harshly. "You saying you weren't?"

"Well, no, sir—I ain't, but I—"

"It was you and Howe that rustled Mrs. Judson's calves last year, too, wasn't it? And the year before that?"

Benjie stood mute and motionless. Sweat covered his face and arms and darkened his clothing. "Yeh," he said finally, in a barely audible voice, "I reckon it was."

"How many calves did you steal?" Rutledge continued, pressing relentlessly.

"Couple dozen—maybe twenty-five—"

"Every year?"

"Yeh—was every year."

"For how many years?"

Benjie frowned, strove to assemble his disordered thoughts. "Four, I reckon. Was since Ed got the notion to do it—make us rich. This time'd be the fifth."

Hetty shook her head. The two men had been stealing her blind as far as her calf crop was concerned, and she'd just let it go, blaming it on wild animals. That realization pointed up all the more her need for a man around the ranch—a husband, actually. She couldn't possibly look after everything.

"We never took more'n a couple a dozen," she heard Benjie say in a whining voice. "Always left a few—more'n we drove off," he added, as if that was something to be chalked up in his favor. "I'm betting there's twenty maybe thirty more of them calves on down below here in that thick brush."

"Did you and Ed get those you were driving from my upper range?" Hetty asked.

"Yes'm, sure did. We always started high up and drove them down, and sort of gathered along the way. Was easy doing it like that."

Rutledge drew his pistol, began to toy with it, carelessly allowing the muzzle to point at Benjie from time to time.

"After you stole the calves what did you do with them?" he asked. "Being in the cattle business you had to have a buyer."

"Oh, sure! We sold them to Mr. Madison, Ed's boss. He took all we drove in and paid us five dollars a head, was they in good shape."

The calves were unbranded, Hetty realized as anger swept through her, but still Cain Madison should have questioned where they came from. The truth would be, of course, that he didn't want to know.

"Didn't Madison ever ask you where you got them?" Rutledge asked, apparently thinking along the same lines.

"No, sir. Just said it didn't make no difference, that we

was to keep driving them in and he'd keep right on paying us for them."

"Was Mrs. Judson the only rancher you've been stealing from?"

"Nope, there's a couple of other places—on south of Mr. Madison's place. He'd only pay us three dollars a head for them, though. They was scrawny, never fat like the ones we got up here."

Hetty swore like a man under her breath as anger continued to course through her. But it was pointless to rage at Cain Madison. She knew the kind of man he was and therefore knew she should not be surprised or upset at what she had learned he was doing. She should instead be grateful to Rutledge for uncovering the rustling and putting a stop to it.

"You've been stealing calves from this lady here for four years, and you say you took a couple of dozen head. We'll settle for twenty-five each time. That tallies up to a hundred calves Madison bought from you."

"I ain't much good at counting, but I reckon that's right if you say so."

"Way I figure it they're worth ten dollars a head now—since they're grown up. Madison probably sold a lot of them off for more—sixteen or eighteen dollars—at the market. But we'll let him off the hook for ten."

"Yes, sir," Benjie said, agreeing.

Hetty frowned, tried to understand what John Rutledge was working up to. She found out moments later.

"That means that Cain Madison owes Mrs. Judson one thousand dollars—that's one hundred calves at ten dollars apiece. Now, I want you to listen and get this straight in your head, Benjie. If you don't do what I tell you and do it right, I'm coming in and getting you. Then I'm string-

ing you up to a tree like we always do rustlers. Not sure
but what I ought to go ahead anyway. Could be you
won't do what I tell—"

"Yes, sir—I sure will!" Benjie shouted. "Just you say
what you want done—and I'll do it!"

Rutledge gave that thought, his cold, flat eyes all the
while on the rustler. Then, "All right. Load up your partner and take him to Madison. When you get there tell
Cain that you and Howe got caught rustling calves from
Mrs. Judson. Understand?"

"Yes, sir—"

"Then you tell him he's already bought a hundred
calves that were stolen from her by you and Howe, and
that he owes Mrs. Judson for them—one thousand dollars.
They're costing him ten dollars a head. Can you remember all that?"

"I sure can—"

"Tell Madison I want him to go to the bank and put
the thousand dollars in Mrs. Judson's account—and I want
it done before dark tomorrow. I aim to ride in then and
talk to the man at the bank. If Madison hasn't done it, I'm
going out and collect from him personally. That clear?"

Benjie bobbed. "If he don't give the bank a thousand
dollars for Mrs. Judson you're going to collect it yourself,"
he said, and as Rutledge nodded confirmation, he turned
at once to Ed Howe.

He was unable to lift the dead man and, after a few futile attempts, glanced appealingly to Rutledge. The tall
rider dismounted and, crossing to where the Circle M
man lay, assisted Benjie in hanging the body over the saddle and securing it.

Hetty, silent, watched as Benjie caught up his own
horse and mounted it. Taking the reins of Howe's buck-

skin, he started to pull away. Rutledge's stern voice checked him.

"You tell Madison everything I said—unless you want to swing for rustling!" he warned.

"I sure will, mister!" Benjie answered, and hurried on.

Hetty, already happily calculating what a thousand dollars cash could do for her, smiled at Rutledge. Having seen him in action she harbored no doubt in her mind that Madison would comply with the demand. The money, as far as she was concerned, was as good as in the bank.

"I won't have to sell off any stock now this year—thanks to you," she said. "Maybe not for the next couple of years. It's wonderful, John, you doing all that you have for me. I don't know how to thank you."

"No need," Rutledge replied with a shrug. "Cain Madison had a good thing going for him—time he started paying for it." He paused, looking down the arroyo. Only three of the calves were visible, the rest having scattered.

"Expect we'd better get back to work," he said, now glancing at the sun. "You'll still want your stock driven down to your lower range and your calves rounded up and branded."

Hetty studied him for a long minute thinking about his dislike for such work. "We can let it go now, John. With all that cash it won't be necessary."

She watched his shoulders stir, saw him look off across the low hills. Finally he said, "No, I started it, might as well finish it. We've already got a big bunch of cows headed in the right direction; now we can roust those calves Benjie and Howe gathered and start them trailing along after them. Could say we're about half done."

Hetty Judson smiled, nodded. "I appreciate this, and I

thank you again—but it's getting on to noon—dinner time. If you'll help me get that bunch of calves together again, I'll drive them ahead of me on my way back to the ranch, get them to following the rest of the herd. Then you do what you like for a bit, and in a couple of hours meet me at that little grove of trees on below here. I'll have sandwiches and coffee for us."

"Sounds fine," he said and, crossing to the brush, caught up Hetty's horse and led it back to her.

She let him assist her onto the saddle, afraid that refusal would offend him. After he had mounted his black, they rode off down the arroyo together. The calves had not strayed far, and within a half hour she was moving up the slope of the slight hill to the east with the small herd noisily complaining ahead of her.

When they topped out and caught sight of the rest of the stock, grazing as they drifted, on the flat below, all broke and began to run, anxious to join others of their kind. At that moment, Hetty turned and looked back. John Rutledge was a distant, silhouetted figure on his black horse doubling back over the trail for the upper range. There, where they had stopped working the brush when they had hurried to investigate the bawling calves, he would resume the roundup.

She felt her pulse quicken as she watched. How could she persuade him to stay? He wasn't interested in becoming a partner much less an ordinary hired hand, and to him marriage was out of the question. The memory of Lacey was still too strong in his mind. But there must be a way—there had to be!

22

When the last of the straying calves the two rustlers had gathered were rounded up and Hetty was on her way with them, Rutledge swung the black about and headed back for the Judsons' upper range. He'd pick up where they had broken off, resuming what was passing as a roundup but in reality was nothing more than popping steers out of the brush.

He smiled wryly. Just how in the hell had he managed to get himself involved in work that he so heartily detested? Under ordinary circumstances no amount of money could have hired him to take on such a back-breaking, disagreeable chore.

Hell—he could sit down to a card game and make more hard cash in a couple of hours playing stud poker than he could in a month of Mondays hazing cows! And if some grudge-bearing, well-heeled rancher came along looking for a hired gun to do a job, and he was in the proper mood to accept the offer as he had been back in south Texas a time earlier—why, in a couple of days he could end up with enough money in his poke to buy a stinking herd!

Then—why?

Rutledge glanced down at the worn, ragged pants, once a pair worn by Jack Judson, which he had pulled on over his own as protection against the thorny brush en-

countered in the overgrown draws. He didn't own a pair
of working chaps and an improvisation had been necessary.

Further, as his stirrups were without leather taps, his
boots now were scarred and dusty and appeared to be
years old rather than fairly new. The jacket he'd pulled
on was ripped and torn as were the gloves he wore. All in
all, he presented the appearance of a down-and-out cowhand at the finish of a hard winter.

Rutledge grinned, tenderly explored the long scratch a
swinging branch had laid across his cheek. He couldn't
answer his own question. He'd simply stepped in and
taken hold of a bad situation without thinking. Half turning, Rutledge produced his bottle of whiskey from its
place in the saddlebags and treated himself to a drink. It
wasn't a case of taking up for a lost cause, he was certain.
He was one who didn't believe in such foolishness—par-
ticularly in one that could be labeled as lost right from
the start.

Nor could it be said that he was inclined to stand up
for the underdog or the downtrodden. John Rutledge was
a firm believer in the premise that a man should fight his
own battles in this world, neither asking for nor giving
quarter, and either living or dying as a result of his own
efforts.

Could Hetty Judson be the answer? Could it be that
she, a woman standing alone against a man like Cain
Madison and doing a hell of a good job of it, was the
reason he had swerved from his usual pattern of life and
taken on a chore he ordinarily would not even have considered?

Hetty did remind him some of Lacey, Rutledge
thought as he topped out one of the countless small knolls

that bubbled across the Judson land. Both were dark-haired, blue-eyed women, tall for their sex and with a vitality that radiated from their shapely bodies and proclaimed their femininity.

That, most logically, explained why he found himself in —frankly—such a predicament, he decided, and again Rutledge grinned wryly at the thought of the reactions of several who knew him should they get a look at him at that moment.

But he reckoned he'd live through a few more days of working for Hetty Judson—unless, of course, one of Cain Madison's hired hands bushwhacked him somewhere along the way; and that would become a distinct possibility when Benjie rode in with Ed Howe's body and informed the rancher that he was to pay for the stolen calves that he'd bought from them.

So what? Rutledge's broad shoulders stirred as he dug out his bottle again and had another pull at the whiskey. He didn't intend to let himself get bushwhacked, and he was fully aware of all the risks involved when he put himself at the top of Cain Madison's hate list. He hadn't thought of it in just that way at the beginning but he guessed that down deep in his mind he was courting danger and excitement and recognizing it as his compensation for taking a hand in Hetty Judson's troubles.

He reached the spur of brush where he and Hetty had earlier halted operations and, sighing heavily, cigar now clamped between his teeth, headed the black into the ragged growth. Such labor—popping stray cattle out of the thickets—was better done by moonlight, but it had been Hetty's wish that it be done now, and so he resumed the dusty, sweaty chore with no small amount of resignation.

He worked steadily at it until the time stated by Hetty

was up and then, hazing the dozen or so steers ahead of him, started back for the small cluster of cottonwoods growing along the creek a half a mile or so to his left. He reached the appointed spot shortly and found the woman awaiting him.

"I was about to start looking for you," she said, smiling.

He pulled the black to a halt a few strides below where Hetty had picketed her mare and swung down. Shucking the dusty outer clothes he was wearing, he stepped up to the creek, washed his face and hands and, drying them with his bandanna, turned back to the woman.

"Got to be honest and tell you that being real interested in the job I was doing isn't why I'm a bit late," he said. "Just took a mite longer than I figured it would. Looks like a Sunday sociable," he added, nodding at the food placed, picnic style, on a cloth under the trees.

"I thought you'd likely be hungry. There's sliced meat, fresh bread, beans, and sweet corn to fill up on. Can top that off with peach pie and coffee. . . . I hope it suits you."

"Can take bets on it," Rutledge said heartily, sitting down at the edge of the cloth. "Everything all right with the little girl?"

"She's fine," Hetty replied. A small frown puckered her brow. "Do you know that I've never heard you call her by name? You always say *the little girl*. Willa would love it if you'd use her name."

Rutledge shrugged. He was a man wary of friendship, never permitted himself to get close to anyone, man, woman, or child, feeling that to do so could lead to complications in the future. Such was only natural; once deeply wounded by fate he could be expected to avoid any possibility of a repeat just as a blacksmith, carelessly burning himself at his forge, became doubly cautious not to let it happen again.

"Sure," he said, but there was nothing definite in the promise. He helped himself to the bread and meat.

Hetty was silent for several moments. Then, "Did you find many more cows up where we stopped working?"

"About a dozen. Pretty well finished with the brush. Doubt if we'll scare up many more. Was no calves."

"Expect Howe and Benjie got all there were along there. Should be some on below."

Rutledge nodded. "Looks like you might end up with a pretty fair calf crop."

"Yes—thanks to you," Hetty said, pausing in the process of quartering the pie. "And thanks to you I'm suddenly in good shape—money-wise, and I've got my herd down where I can manage it." She hesitated and, head inclined, looked closely at him. "John, is there any use in asking you again to stay on? You—we could make a wonderful life here together—the two of us—if you—"

Rutledge shook his head, cutting off her hesitant words. Lowering the cup of coffee he was holding, he returned her gaze.

"Any man would take your offer as a mighty big compliment—and it is," he said. "But for us it plain wouldn't work out. I know myself, and one thing I've always taken pride in is being honest with myself as well as other folks —specially the ones I like. I'd end up making you miserable—mainly because I'd be miserable."

"But maybe you'd find it different here—and not like the other ranches where you've worked! You—you'd be the owner, if you wanted. I really think if you'd try, give it—us—a chance."

"The difference would be here, all right—but I'd be the

same. That's where the rub would come in. No, it's best I move on soon as things are squared away for you. Another day working your range ought to take care of rounding up your stock, and then I'll need to ride into town, see for certain that Madison has put that thousand dollars he owes you for those calves into your account at the bank.

"Once that's done, I'll be heading out. If Farwell sent off some telegrams asking about me—and I'm pretty sure he did—he'll start getting his answers about this time and—"

John Rutledge's voice trailed off, and his eyes, as he stared off into the distance, narrowed to cut down the glare. Pointing to a dark smudge hanging in the sky to the east, he said: "That smoke—is it coming from your place?"

Hetty swung her attention to the direction he had indicated. A cry escaped her lips as she leaped to her feet.

"It is!" she said, hoarsely. "Something's wrong!"

23

Wheeling instantly, Hetty ran to her horse. Yanking the reins free of the brush clump to which they had been attached, she lunged up onto the saddle and was rushing off even before her feet had settled in the stirrups. Rutledge, grim, was only a stride behind her, and shortly side by side they were racing toward the ominous cloud of black smoke hanging in the sky above her ranch.

"You think it could be Madison?" Hetty shouted to the tall rider. Her features were drawn, anxious, and her eyes bespoke the fear for Willa that gripped her.

"Hard to guess. Could be a brush fire that got started somehow," he replied. "And I reckon it could be him. His kind aim to get their way no matter what it takes."

Hetty brushed at her eyes. "Always knew Cain was a cold-hearted, greedy man but I never thought he'd drop low enough to use a child to—"

"If it's him," Rutledge cut in, hoping to ease her worry. "We get close enough we best go in quiet, have ourselves a look and see what it's all about."

Hetty nodded, again swiped at her eyes. "If they—if he's hurt Willa—I'll kill him—I'll kill him myself!"

Rutledge made no comment and moments later they topped out the last rise to the west of the ranch buildings and came to a full view of the place. The fire was coming from one of the sheds in the yard behind the house. Brush had been dragged in from nearby, piled about the wooden structure and set afire. As most of the growth used was green, a thick column of black smoke had risen to hang motionless overhead.

"It's not the house—so I guess Willa is all right," Hetty said with a long sigh. "I wonder where she is?"

Keeping behind the rising bulk of the barn and the lines of brush that stood as winglike windbreaks off its sides, Hetty and Rutledge moved in quietly. A half a dozen men could be seen, scattered about the yard so as to have it well covered. There was no sign of Madison or, as Hetty had noted, of her small daughter.

Rutledge frowned, rubbed at the sweat on his jaw as he struggled to puzzle out the scene. Cain Madison's big white horse was tied to the hitch rack at the rear of the house; where was the rancher?

There was movement beyond the kitchen's screen door —shadowy, struggling figures. Rutledge halted, reached for Hetty's arm, brought her to a stop. Suddenly the door, as if kicked, flung open. A man came out onto the porch. He was carrying a squirming child in his arms. It took no second glance to see that it was Madison and that he was holding Willa.

"He's—he's got my daughter!" Hetty moaned, and jamming her spurs into her horse, started forward.

Quick, Rutledge seized her reins, checked the mare she was riding before it could get underway.

"Wait," he counseled. "See what he wants."

"I don't care what he wants! He can have it all—everything I've got just as long as he doesn't hurt my little girl!" Hetty's voice was high, almost hysterical.

"He won't," Rutledge assured her quietly. "I'll put a bullet through his head if he makes the slightest move to lay a hand on her. Be an easy target for me from here. Let's see what he's up to."

"It's not hard to figure that out," Hetty said bitterly. "He wants me to give in to him—quit my ranch, let him take over."

"Still be smart to hear him out. Maybe we can come up with a—"

"What've you got there, boss—a little wildcat?"

The shouted question came from one of the rancher's hired hands standing off to one side in the yard.

Madison had moved to the edge of the porch, was holding Willa about the waist in front of him as if she were a shield. The girl was still kicking and twisting about in an effort to break free but the rancher's strong arms encircled her slight body and her wild flailing was to no avail. Madison and his riders must have sneaked up on her, Rutledge realized, and gained entrance to the house before she saw them, as there had not been any warning rifle shots.

"You want me to hang onto her for you, Mr. Madison?"

The rancher shook his head. "Nope, I can handle one small kid. It won't be for long, anyway. Her ma'll be showing up fast when she spots all that smoke."

Rutledge came down off his horse, motioned for Hetty to do likewise. Securing the animals to a clump of sumac, he turned to her.

"I want you to go out there and show yourself—but don't get any closer to him than the edge of the yard," he said. "Find out what he wants—we know, but make him spell it out. I need time to circle around and get into the house. The way he's got his men scattered around, I've got to come in behind him without being seen."

"Time—how much?" Hetty asked nervously.

"Ten, maybe fifteen minutes. Watch the back door. That's where you'll see me when I've made it." He started to pivot, hurry off, but paused. "If things get out of hand —with Madison, I mean—I'll know it but just in case I'm not where I can see, give me a signal anyway."

Hetty nodded her understanding and at once Rutledge continued, slipping off into the brush and making his way toward the front of the house. He moved slowly and carefully, keeping his passage as quiet as possible since, more than likely, Cain Madison had other men waiting in ambush as an extra precaution. Shortly he heard Hetty Judson's voice, firm and clear, break the hush.

"I'm here, Madison! But I'll tell you first off, you hurt my daughter and I'll kill you if it's the last thing on this earth that I do!"

Rutledge, dropping low, made his way to the fringe of the brush. Hetty was standing at the edge of the ragged windbreak, rifle cradled in her arms.

"Now, she ain't going to get hurt," Madison called back, "leastwise, it ain't likely if me and you comes to terms."

Rutledge grinned tightly as he resumed his progress through the brush. Hetty was carrying it off just as he'd hoped. The one thing that could set her off, however, force her to do something rash would be for the rancher to actually cause the child pain.

"Terms?" Hetty echoed. "What's that mean? That a new word for knuckling under to you?"

"It means whatever you want it to," Madison answered coolly. "You want this youngun of yours back without getting hurt—accidentally, of course—then you'll listen to me—and do damn well what I tell you to!"

"Let's hear it, Madison—"

Rutledge smiled again, bleakly. Hetty Judson was not backing down; she was making a show of holding her own against Cain Madison, although she was wracked with fear for her daughter's safety. Realization came to him at that moment; she was trusting him completely to let no harm come to her small daughter—and he fully intended to live up to that trust.

"First off, I want that jasper you hired on—I think he's called Rutledge. He's gone and killed another of my hands—shot him down in cold blood."

"Wasn't that way at all!" Hetty declared, angrily. "I was right there, saw it all. Ed Howe went for his gun after John—Rutledge—warned him not to try."

"Well, it don't make no difference," Madison said, shrugging. "Howe's dead, and so's my boy Clint, along with a couple other good men. He's a killer and I want him—"

"For what? You turning him over to the law?"

"I'm my own law in this part of Texas," the rancher said. "I aim to deal with him myself."

"That all you want—just him?"

"Not by a damn sight! You're mixed up with Rutledge in them killings but I'll overlook that long as you pack up and get out. I've got the papers right here in my pocket for you to sign."

"I'm to just turn my ranch over to you, that it?"

"That's it—along with Rutledge."

"Let's just leave him out of this. He's got nothing to do with any deal you and I might make," Hetty snapped. "I won't tell you where he is and I won't ask him to give himself up. He'll have to decide himself what he wants to do."

"Sounds like he's hiding out—"

Hetty forced a laugh. "John Rutledge hiding out from you? You know better, Madison!"

"Then where the hell is he? Was told he was with you on your range."

"He was—and he's around somewhere—close. Don't make the mistake of thinking he's not."

That Hetty was doing her utmost to stall, to permit him to reach the position he had in mind, was apparent to Rutledge. He hoped she could keep the rancher's attention for a bit longer.

"Well, he sure better be showing up," Madison said, taking a firmer grip on Willa.

He had allowed her to slide through his arms to the point where her feet now touched the floor of the porch, thus relieving the strain on his muscles, but he showed no inclination to release her as yet.

"What about the rest of what I said? You willing to get out, let me have this place?"

"Just plain hand it over to you?"

"There'll be a thousand dollars waiting for you at the bank. I don't figure I have to pay you a dime, but I ain't so hardhearted that I'd turned a woman and her kid out dead flat broke."

"You saying you'll pay a thousand dollars to me for my ranch?"

"Yes'm—just because I'm feeling right generous."

"Generous—poppycock!" Hetty laughed scornfully. "You already owe me that thousand for those calves of mine that you—"

"That's more than poppycock—that's bull!" Madison broke in. "I don't owe you nothing, woman, and if you keep on bucking and ragging me, I won't give you nothing. I'll just go ahead and take—"

"That's what you been doing all along," Rutledge heard Hetty reply in a dry voice. "There's nothing new in that. Why don't you let my little girl go? You don't need her to talk this over."

"I ain't about to turn her loose—she's my ace in the hole! And we're plumb finished talking things over. Either you say yes to what I'm telling you, or my boys start in taking this here hardscrabble outfit apart. Aim to pull down everything that's standing and put the torch to it. And while they're real busy doing it I ain't going to be responsible for what might happen to your kid—or you."

"You're a real brave man—using a helpless child to get what you want!" Hetty screamed the words at the rancher.

"It's the reason I'm big like I am," Madison replied. "I got one rule—I do whatever I have to to get what I want. I don't let nobody stand in my way once I've got my mind made up."

"Well, you better not hurt her—not even a little scratch! I've warned you, Cain Madison—and I'll do what I said—I'll kill you for sure if—"

Madison's laugh cut into the woman's words. "Now, just what do you think my boys'll be doing if you even raise that gun you're holding?" he asked. "You reckon they'll let you draw a bead on me? Not much! The second you try, you're dead."

"Maybe so—but how'll you explain killing me to Tom Farwell and the other folks around here?"

"Won't have to. Like I said, I'm the law here. Anyway, you're the one that'll be making the first move. My boys'll only be protecting me—keeping you from shooting me. Self-defense, they call it.

"But the hell with that! I'm done talking. I want your answer right now. Either you tell me what I want to hear or I signal my boys to go to work. What's it going to be?"

24

It was still a long hundred feet to where he could cross open ground unseen and enter the house by its front door, Rutledge saw, but the situation in the yard was becoming desperate for Hetty. He recognized this in the impatient note sharpening Madison's tone. The rancher could reach the end of his rope at any moment and direct his men to start carrying out his threat.

But Rutledge also knew that it could be a mistake to hurry, to ignore the men he was certain were lurking about in the brush; and, he could by thoughtless action set off Madison himself, start a chain of violence that could result in injury or death for Hetty and her small daughter.

Taut, moving with extreme care, he continued, taking each step slowly, avoiding the dry brush that could rattle and warn someone nearby of his presence. He caught sight of a Circle M man just off to his left as he drew nearer to the front of the house, and instantly ducked lower. The rider's attention was centered on the yard. Rutledge took a deeper breath and, a gun in his left hand, moved on.

He covered no more than a dozen steps when he again drew to a stop. Another of Cain Madison's men caught the tail of his eye. It was Dave Hollander. He recognized Madison's foreman immediately. Dave was also between him and the yard. Like the other Madison rider, he was concentrating on the activity in the yard behind the house.

Rutledge, scarcely breathing, sweat now clothing his lank body, continued, picking each step with utmost care. Once beyond Hollander it was likely there'd be no more Circle M men; Madison would have staked them out where they would have a clear view of the porch at the rear of the ranch house and the lower end of the yard where he, Rutledge smiled at the realization, was expected to appear.

"What about it?" Madison's voice was harsh, demanding. "Time's up. Either you say yes or I start burning down this crow's nest!"

There followed a silence broken only by the buzzing of a cicada in a nearby tree. Rutledge reached it and, as the noisy insect hushed at his approach, paused to hear Hetty's reply. He was not quite even with the back of the house yet and had that small distance plus the length of the structure to cover before he'd be able to cross and enter. Once that was accomplished—if he could manage it unnoticed—he needed only to move quickly through the house to reach the back porch—and Cain Madison.

"I can't give you my answer—not until I see John Rutledge and talk it over with him," Hetty said.

She was still hoping to stall while at the same time warning him, Rutledge knew. There was no need to discuss anything with him; it was a question that was entirely up to her. Quickening his steps as much as he dared, Rutledge moved on.

"Then, by God—you get him up here!"

"He's off on the range working—I'm not sure where."

Hetty was buying him time, moment by moment, as best she could.

"How do you call him in? You got a iron bar or something you bang on when you want him to come eat?"

Rutledge had reached the lilac bushes that were level with the front of the house. He glanced around, saw no one near, and quickly crossed from the brush to the thickly leafed shrubs. Gaining them, he paused for breath, and then stepped up onto the porch.

"Two gunshots—that's the signal I use when I want him in a hurry—"

Hetty had gone as far as she could; she had kept Cain Madison at bay long enough for him to reach the front door of the house. Now it was up to him. Still quiet, he hurriedly crossed the porch, reached the entrance. At that moment two gunshots broke the hush, stilling the cicada again and sending a pair of wild pigeons flapping erratically off toward the trees to the south.

"He sure better show up now!" Madison's voice was at a high level and trembled with anger as if it had dawned upon him that Hetty Judson had been stringing him along. "I'm plumb out of patience with you, woman!"

Rutledge turned to the door. It was open, blocked by a chair that had been placed against it to prevent its closing. He frowned. That was none of Hetty's or the little girl's doing; in the interest of good housekeeping, screens were always kept shut.

"What the hell—"

John Rutledge lashed out instantly with the pistol in his hand. He had not seen the man standing just inside the doorway, stationed there by Madison—nor had the rider seen or heard him until he had taken that first step into the room.

The blow, delivered with the speed and accuracy of a striking rattler, caught the Circle M man across the forehead, sent him reeling against the wall and then into a small table placed against it. Rutledge leaped forward to catch the rider and prevent his fall and the disturbance such would create. He managed to do that much, but the table tipped, spilling the books that were on it to the floor.

Rutledge cursed silently. Holding the unconscious man by one arm, he lowered him gently while listening for some indication that the racket had been heard. But there was no questioning call, no sound of anyone hurrying up to investigate.

Pulling the man's weapon from its holster, Rutledge tossed it into the dead ashes of the fireplace, and now, with both forty-fives drawn and ready, crossed the room and made his way swiftly to the kitchen and to the door—also propped open—that let out onto the back porch.

"You're horsing me around, woman!" The rancher's voice was still high, reflected even more anger and impatience. "Where is he?"

"Right here, Madison," Rutledge said, and stepped into the doorway.

The rancher whirled. Willa, brushed aside by his knee in the sudden motion, fell. She was back up in an instant and racing across the yard to her mother.

"You—damn you—I—" Madison yelled, glaring at Rutledge. The tall rider's unexpected nearness had completely unnerved him and now, eyes glittering with hate, face contorted and flushed, he was beside himself with anger. "Shoot him! Damn it—shoot him!"

Rutledge saw a man beyond the rancher go for his pistol. He brought up his own weapon and fired. The rider staggered and fell. In that same moment Madison had lunged to one side, had dragged out the pistol he carried, and was leveling it.

Rutledge, half in, half out of the doorway, fired from the hip. The rancher buckled, caught himself, struggled to get off a shot. Rutledge triggered his weapon again, and then, as Madison dropped heavily to the floor of the porch, shifted his attention back to the yard and the men there.

Through the drifting powder smoke from his guns he saw that there were now but two in sight—and they, like their friends, were hurrying toward the brush on the far side of the cleared area. Hetty, small daughter in her arms, was crouched low close to the side of the barn where she had sought refuge from stray bullets.

There was the shadow of a smile on Rutledge's taut lips. Eyes glowing with a brightness that bordered on joy, a leveled and cocked pistol in each hand, he moved out onto the porch. Crossing slowly to the platform's edge, he halted and glanced about.

"All right, who's next?" he challenged. "Your boss is a dead man but I reckon there's room in hell for you, too, if you want to try your hand! Step out and—"

"No!" The voice came from the side of the house. "Don't a manjack of you touch your gun! This here's Tom Farwell ordering it."

Farwell, the town marshal—the man who professed to have no authority, legally or morally, outside the town limits of Jubilee.

"You all hear me?" the lawman continued. "I'm telling you to holster your guns and walk out there into the yard where I can see you. Means you, too, Rutledge! Now, I ain't fooling. I've got four deputies with rifles backing me up!"

Dave Hollander was the first to appear, coming out of the brush and into the yard while Farwell was still speaking. Two more Circle M riders appeared, and then a half a dozen others. All had complied with the marshal's order to put away their weapons and were glancing warily at Rutledge, standing rigid and unyielding on the porch.

"Rutledge—you hear me?"

"I heard you, Marshal," the tall rider replied.

His eyes were on the opposite side of the yard where Hetty was conversing with a man who was holding a rifle. It was Granville, the storekeeper, he saw. Elsewhere around the clearing other similarly equipped men were appearing—Pete Zell, the saloonkeeper was one; the others, undoubtedly Jubilee merchants, were strangers.

"Then do what I told you—put them guns away and step out in the open. . . . No, maybe you best just unbuckle your gunbelt, let it fall, then come out."

"I'm not about to do that. I keep my guns."

Farwell was silent. He was still along the side of the house and not visible to Rutledge. "All right," he said, finally, "but you sure better know this—there'll be rifles pointed at you every step you take. Make a wrong move and my deputies'll shoot. . . . You hear that, men? Keep your rifles on him!"

Rutledge saw Zell and the others raise their weapons, level them at him. He considered their movements coldly for a time, and then, shrugging, slid his pistols into their holsters and strolled indifferently into the center of the yard.

Suddenly, Tom Farwell, standing at the corner of the

house and now in a position to get a full look at Rutledge, swore deeply.

"I knew it—knew I was right! You ain't somebody named Rutledge—you're Ringo—John Ringo!"

25

The man wheeled slowly in the sudden hush that had fallen over the yard. Features set and completely devoid of expression, he faced the lawman.

"So—"

Farwell glanced about as if to reassure himself that Ringo was well covered. The deputized merchants who had accompanied him had done as ordered. Madison's riders were now gathered in a tight group and talking back and forth in a low-pitched, excited sort of way. Hetty Judson, holding to her small daughter with one hand, rifle in the other, was hurrying up from the barn.

"Knew dang well that first day I laid eyes on you that I'd seen you somewheres before," Farwell said. "Got busy and sent out a couple of telegrams just to sort of back my hunch. One I ain't heard from yet but the other'n answered. Mailed me a Ranger-wanted dodger—got it this morning by the stage." The lawman paused, nodded. "It's sure a good picture of you, Ringo."

The tall rider shrugged. "Thought you said you never bothered with something that happened outside your town. Claimed you didn't have any authority. If that's true, what are you doing here?"

"That shooting in town yesterday—that's why. I warned you plain—"

"Was no fault of mine. Madison's hired gun came looking for me."

"And you wasn't about to dodge him! But I reckon you never do something like that. You mostly're hunting for trouble, not dodging it."

"Probably so," Ringo drawled. "I was looking for you to step in yesterday and stop the shoot-out—but you'd found yourself a reason to leave town."

Farwell snorted angrily. "You saying I rode off a'purpose so's I wouldn't be there?"

Ringo's wide shoulders stirred. Hetty had come up to him, after sending Willa into the house, and was standing beside him.

"I reckon you can answer that better than anybody else," he said.

Tom Farwell brushed at the sweat on his leathery face, turned to Hollander. "Dave, have a couple of your boys get Madison and Dan Tolliver out of here," he directed, motioning at the dead men. "Best they tote them into town and turn them over to Harry Winslow for burying."

Hollander nodded, spoke to the men grouped about him. Four moved off at once toward the sprawled figures of Madison and the rider who had attempted to shoot it out with Ringo.

"Well, if you're wanting to know where I was," Farwell resumed, "I rode out to Madison's place. Could see that real bad trouble was shaping up and I was hoping to talk him into backing off. Didn't have no luck."

The lawman paused and watched as the bodies of the rancher and the man called Tolliver were loaded across the saddles of their horses, which were brought in from the brush north of the yard and then led away.

"Heard about the shooting when I got back. Wasn't

much I could do, it being all done and over with. Then I got this dodger on the stage this morning and I figure I had to do something and had to do it quick—you being who you are. Got some of the merchants together, hashed it over, deputized them that was willing to help—and we lit out for here aiming to stop any more murders."

"Not murders," Ringo corrected softly. "They tried to go up against me and didn't make it. They went for their guns first."

Farwell again brushed at the sweat on his face, glancing at Hollander. "You see it, Dave?"

The Circle M foreman nodded. "Sure did and what he said about going for iron first's right—but I still think it's murder. Madison or Tolliver never had a chance against him—and he knew that. Goes for all the others he's killed —they were murdered."

"No!" Hetty Judson shouted, taking a step toward Hollander. "He warned them not to try and shoot it out with him. He told them all straight out that he'd kill them if they did. They went ahead anyway—and failed. You can't call that murder!"

"He's a professional killer—a hired gun," Hollander said, doggedly.

"I don't see where that makes any difference. He warned them. It's their fault if they didn't believe and wanted to take a chance."

Farwell smiled condescendingly at the woman. "You just don't savvy these things, Mrs. Judson. Best you—"

"I understand, all right!" Hetty shot back. "You're trying to say John Rutledge is a cold-blooded killer. It's not so! I know him for a kind and gentle man who stepped in and helped me when nobody else—none of you—would!"

"But Mrs. Judson, you've got—"

"He went right to work doing a job I knew he hated when he could've just ridden on. And then when Cain Madison and his bunch tried to run over him, he fought back in the only way he could. But even when the odds were all against him, he gave them a warning. Told them he'd kill them because they were no match for him. I'm grateful to—"

"Mrs. Judson!" Farwell shouted to break through the words pouring from Hetty. "Hell a mighty, woman—you don't seem to realize who you're talking about! This man's not John Rutledge like he said—he's John Ringo—likely the worst and deadliest killer in the whole state!"

Hetty shook her head stubbornly. "Names don't count for much—it's what's inside a man that does. He's good and he's kind. That much I know for certain and he did what he had to when he faced up to Cain Madison and his bunch."

"That's maybe how you look at him," Farwell said, resignedly. "Truth is, he's a killer. There's a long list of shooting scrapes he's got hisself into and it ain't only the Rangers wanting to talk to him but a half a dozen sheriffs and marshals, too. Just before he rode into here he was in jail down Mason County way for murder."

Ringo's eyes narrowed slightly. "Tell the rest of it, Farwell—"

The lawman once again brushed at the sweat on his face, again looked around the yard at the silent men. "He was turned loose. Happened he was in jail somewheres else when the killing took place. But that don't prove nothing. There's plenty other men he shot down that he ain't been hung or sent to jail for. That's what the law wants to talk to him about. You deny that, Ringo?"

"No," Ringo replied in his soft, cool way. "But I've

never killed a man yet who wasn't trying to kill me first."

Granville, the general store owner, and the other deputized merchants had moved in closer and were now standing close by. All but one had lowered their rifles.

"I think maybe we're pushing this man too hard, Tom," the storekeeper said. "Could even say we're persecuting him for things that happened in the past and that we sure've got no right to judge him for. And far as now's concerned, what he's told us was the truth; he only protected himself."

Farwell bristled. "You want him—his kind—hanging around Jubilee shooting and killing?"

"No, of course we don't. But if he's willing to ride on—"

"There's warrants out for his arrest. I get them, it's my sworn duty to jail him—"

"You do, Marshal, and I'll go straight to Austin and tell the governor the whole story!" Hetty declared angrily, her voice lifting. "I'll tell him how John was the only man around who had the courage to help me, to stand up to Cain Madison—and he did that knowing he was risking his chance for escape from the law. I didn't understand that at the time it came up, but I do now."

"What you just said goes to prove that the law wants him," Farwell pointed out. "That how it is, Ringo? You running from the law when you showed up here?"

Ringo smiled briefly. "Not exactly running, Marshal, but I'll admit there are a few tin stars wanting to talk to me. Can't say that I was taking any special pains to avoid them, however."

Farwell stirred, spat. "Nope, I expect you wouldn't. Suit you more to shoot it out with them. That's your way of handling all your problems—with a six gun."

"Day comes to a man when that's the only answer he can afford. . . . You say you aim to lock me up?"

The lawman combed his beard thoughtfully with long fingers. Then, "Seems I'm sort of outvoted on that. I reckon all I've got to say to you is ride on—get out of my town and stay out—starting right now!"

Ringo stiffened perceptibly and a hard smile pulled at the corners of his mouth. "You're covering a lot of ground, Marshal. I'm not ready to move on—"

He paused, feeling Hetty Judson's hand on his arm. Looking down at her, he saw not only appeal in her eyes but a weary resignation as if she were being forced again to abandon another dream.

"Please, John—"

She had seen enough trouble and, for his sake, wanted no more. He studied her upturned face for a long breath, shrugged, brought his attention back to Tom Farwell.

"Whatever you say, Marshal—"

The lawman's sigh of relief was audible. Pete Zell, Granville, and the other merchants relaxed visibly while Hollander and the Circle M riders still present nodded approval.

"One thing," Ringo said, bringing a quick hush back to the yard, "I want it understood that the lady here won't ever again have any trouble getting help."

"You can depend on it," Granville said, and looked down. "Was Madison's doing—and for the sake of business we let him get away with it."

"And there's a little matter of Madison owing her a thousand dollars. Like to know for sure that'll be taken care of."

"A thousand dollars!" Farwell echoed, and glanced at Hollander. "What for?"

"He was buying calves that had been rustled from the lady's herd," Ringo said, supplying the answer. "He knew about it—I sent him the bill."

The dry humor was lost on Farwell. He nodded to Hollander. "That right, Dave?"

The Circle M foreman said, "That's right. Can say Cain owed Mrs. Judson."

"Then there ain't no reason why she can't be paid?"

"No, I'll see to it myself."

Farwell swung back to Ringo. "That satisfy you?"

The tall rider smiled faintly. "I figure Hollander for an honest man. I'll take his word."

"Good! There ain't no reason then why you can't mount up and be on your way."

Ringo looked again at Hetty Judson. "No, I reckon not."

The lawman smiled apologetically. "I'm sort of hoping you savvy my position. It's just that I don't want no more shootings—killings around here. There's been more of that since you hit town than we've had in ten years. Seems you just sort of draw it—like a tall tree draws lightning."

Ringo scarcely heard, his eyes still on Hetty. "Expect you'll get along fine now."

She nodded. "Expect so. I—I don't know how to thank you."

"You already have. Being around you was the best thing to happen to me in a long time. I'm the one to be grateful."

"It won't hurt none if he stays here till morning will it, Tom?" It was Pete Zells's voice. "Day's most gone."

Farwell gave that thought, said, "No, maybe it wouldn't but I'd sure rest a lot easier if he'd move on. There's a few around here," the lawman added, glancing pointedly in the direction of the Circle M riders, "who just might get to mulling things over in their heads and decide they'd like to square things up for their friends. Now, if he'd pull out now there likely wouldn't be no chance of that happening."

Zell said, "Yeh, you're right again, Tom."

Ringo, overhearing, turned from Hetty and faced the lawman and the others.

"Don't fret over it. It'll only take me a couple of minutes to get my gear," he said dryly, jerking a thumb in the direction of the bunkhouse. Pivoting on a heel, he crossed the yard to the low-roofed structure that he had occupied.

When he reappeared, he detoured to the side of the barn, caught up the reins of his horse, and securing the leather bags and slicker-wrapped blanket roll to the saddle, swung aboard. Cutting the black about, he returned to the group standing quietly at the rear of the Judson house. Coldly ignoring the others, Ringo halted before Hetty.

"Was a real pleasure knowing you," he said quietly and, touching the brim of his hat with a forefinger, turned to ride out of the yard. Midway, he slowed, looked back over a shoulder, pale eyes again settling on the woman.

"Tell the little girl—Willa—so long for me," he said, and rode on.

AUTHOR'S NOTE

This book is based on an unsubstantiated
incident in the life of the legendary
outlaw Johnny Ringo. With the exception
of the principal, the places and characters
involved are purely fictional.